WICHITA TOWN TAMER

The citizens of Wichita are desperate to appoint a lawman who can control the wild Texas cowboys fresh off the trail, and crooked plotters who want to take over the town. Bear River Cal Bonner has earned an enviable reputation as a town tamer, and soon brings peace to the cow town. But his enemies are determined that the saying 'Anything Goes' will be resurrected, and bring in a hired gunman to challenge the marshal. Will the town once again fall into the hands of the unscrupulous bad hats?

DALE GRAHAM

WICHITA TOWN TAMER

Complete and Unabridged

LINFORD
Leicester

First published in Great Britain in 2016 by
Robert Hale
an imprint of The Crowood Press
Wiltshire

First Linford Edition
published 2018
by arrangement with
The Crowood Press
Wiltshire

A catalogue record for this book is available
from the British Library.

ISBN 978–1–4448–3821–3

Published by
F. A. Thorpe (Publishing)
Anstey, Leicestershire

Set by Words & Graphics Ltd.
Anstey, Leicestershire
Printed and bound in Great Britain by
T. J. International Ltd., Padstow, Cornwall

This book is printed on acid-free paper

1

Anything Goes!

Marshal Cal Bonner was fast asleep in the jailhouse. His breathing was steady and even. A loose smile etched a thin line across the rugged contours of his face. He was dreaming about a far more enticing smile offered by one of Cody Meek's gals. Candy Flowers was chief croupier at the Prairie Dog saloon and that grateful 'come-on' look hinted of more to come if'n he played his cards right.

'How's . . . about . . . it . . . then . . . Candy?'

The murmured appeal slurred out even though the marshal's eyes remained tight shut. One of Candy's friends had been rescued by the lawman from the unwanted lascivious attentions of some Texas cowboys. The two culprits were now resident in the cell block awaiting payment of fines by their fuming ramrod.

Cal had chosen to remain in the jail overnight due to threats made by sympathetic pals from the Lazy K outfit. Their herd of 2,000 longhorns were grazing outside town awaiting transfer to the stock yards. Although he carried two pistols and was prepared to employ them, Cal preferred the use of less terminal methods if at all possible. Such tactics had proved extremely effective against the wild antics of the boisterous Texans. The two rannigans now lying comatose in the cell block bore the bruises testifying to the marshal's diligence in upholding the law.

Wichita had only recently attracted a spur of the Atchison, Topeka Railroad that had effectively opened it up to the burgeoning cattle industry. The plan was to extend the line all the way down to Santa Fe in New Mexico territory. The cattle stockyards were now closer for the drovers coming up the Chisholm Trail from Texas. As the attraction of cow towns like Abilene, Ellsworth and Newton had faded, so Wichita's star was in the ascendant, at least until it was usurped by another cow town. But it was to be three years before Dodge City became known as the 'Babylon of the Trail'.

The name Wichita originated from the Indian tribe who occupied the flats adjoining the Arkansas River more than 4,000 years before. In the fifteenth century, Spanish conquistadores under the leadership of Vasquez de Coronado had decimated them. Since then there had always been some form of settlement here.

As the frontier moved steadily westwards, Wichita was always regarded as a tough prairie town. A minor trading post along the Chisholm Trail for the endless herds heading north. Only a year before Cal arrived, the place had been nothing but a loose collection of wooden shacks and tents. But without money in their pockets, the cowboys were eager to push on to the trail's end. That was now Wichita.

By 1872 the town was wide open. Signs posted at both ends of Kingman Street declared that 'Anything goes in Wichita'. Once they were paid off the cowboys spent freely. Every kind of iniquitous entertainment was on offer to cowpokes denied the chance to let off steam during the three-month trek north.

But for the permanent residents there were distinct drawbacks.

Endless supplies of hard liquor, gambling and girls in abundance were provided by traders intent on making their fortunes while the boom lasted. With guns being freely loosed off, places like Wichita proved decidedly hazardous for respectable citizens. Prosperity was all very well, but continued good health demanded that some form of order be established. The two opposing factions needed a compromise.

A town marshal was the answer. In exchange for law and order, the saloons, gambling halls, cat houses and theatres had to pay an enhanced premium for the privilege of remaining in business. It was a small price to pay when such high profits were at stake.

But only the toughest, or the most foolhardy accepted such a death-defying job. Hurricane Bob Selman was of the latter persuasion. The burly cowboy had stayed on after a drive. But he was drunk as a skunk when signing up to allegedly uphold the fragmentary law. And so was the lawyer who administered the contract. It was inevitable that Selman favoured his own kind over the regular citizens. Shootings increased and the whole place was like a scene from the Devil's playground. The situation could not continue without some form of blow-out.

The running down of a youngster by rampaging cowboys charging down Kingman was the straw that broke the camel's back. Selman was sacked. But who could be brought in to replace him? The town council needed a resilient guy, but a steady and reliable one who recognized the law as a means of keeping firm order.

At an emergency council meeting, the name of Bear River Cal Bonner was mentioned by the mayor, who had just returned from a business trip to Abilene. Bonner was at that time a deputy town marshal working under the auspices of the legendary Wild Bill Hickok. But his job had become redundant since the town's heyday as a rip-roaring cow town had faded. Two paid officers were not required anymore. So it was last in first out.

'This guy has already tamed four towns and he comes highly recommended,' intoned the mayor eagerly. 'Anybody selected to work alongside Wild Bill has to be good. As mayor I suggest we offer him the job of town marshal here in Wichita.'

A heated discussion followed. There were those on the council who did not welcome a tough lawman. Any clampdown on the wayward Texans could severely dent their profits being paid into the bank. A vote was finally held. The decision was close but the appointment of Cal Bonner was adjudged to have won.

Cody Meek was not one of those who joined in the cheering that followed. He stamped out of the meeting. A dark scowl marred the urbane persona he normally espoused. The sartorial Meek ran the Prairie Dog saloon, which was the most popular with the free-spending cowpunchers. His absence from the celebrations was not missed. Mayor Wishart and his supporters were well pleased with the result of the vote. Democracy had won the day. Perhaps now the town could move into a more respectable phase and thus merit its upgrading to city status.

Later that day, a cable was despatched to Abilene offering the job of town marshal to Cal Bonner. It was accepted within the hour.

Cal had earned his spurs in the rough and ready gold mining townships of Colorado. It all started when he accepted the job of end-of-track railroad trouble-shooter for the Union Pacific in Wyoming. His primary job was to keep order among the workers. But Cal was more concerned with sharks who were intent on fleecing the track labourers of their hard-earned wages. When one of their comrades was lynched by a vigilante mob for an alleged murder at Bear River, Bonner led a protest in retaliation.

The gun battle that followed led to the town being burned to the ground. Although Bonner supported the workers, he managed to keep both sides of the fracas apart long enough for an army contingent from Fort Bridger to establish firm control. This brave and resourceful action led to him being labelled 'Bear River'.

With his reputation established, Cal Bonner was in great demand. He moved south to clear up mining settlements in Colorado. His polite yet heavy-fisted approach was instrumental in taming such boom towns as Tin Cup, Crested Butte and Bonanza. But it was only when he was appointed as a deputy to Wild Bill Hickok that his reputation as a town tamer become well known throughout the frontier territories.

Between times in Wichita there had been no law to curb the excesses of the recalcitrant Texas cowpokes. With their pockets bulging with greenbacks, the young tearaways were eager for a good time. Shootouts were commonplace. Most were instigated by too much hard liquor. 'Anything Goes' was no idle boast. The citizens were more than ready for some peace and quiet — if such could ever be the lot of a booming cow town.

The arrival of Bear River Cal by train was, therefore, keenly anticipated. The mayor and a couple of town councillors were on the platform to greet him. Cody Meek was not among them. The man who stepped down off the train was a handsome six-footer with broad shoulders and hands as big as plates. He was clean shaven with a chiselled jaw. A straight back and no-nonsense demeanour lent him an imposing air of authority. Blue-grey eyes twinkled adding a jaunty air of mystery.

It was a positive and convincing first impression.

Mayor Henry Wishart stepped forward. 'Are we glad to see you, Mr Bonner,' the panting guy gushed holding out a hand. It was engulfed by a bear-like paw. The mayor winced then quickly introduced his two associates. 'This town needs a firm hand to bring these young punks into line.' He shook his own appendage back to life.

'And we reckon you're the man to do it,' interjected a stout well-dressed man with a stethoscope slung round his neck. 'Doc Bailey at your service. Welcome to Wichita.'

The cheery greeting was accompanied by a loud hail of shouting on the far side of the railroad station. It had emanated from one of the numerous saloons. Three pairs of nervous eyes flicked towards the sound of mayhem. Raucous bellows of drunken hilarity were followed almost at once by a little Chinaman who came running out of the Oriental saloon. Two swaying cowboys emerged holding a snipped pigtail in the air. 'You want this back, Chow Ling?' one drawled, waving his smoking pistol around. 'It'll cost you ten bucks.' His pal joined in the rampant guffawing as, arm in arm, they staggered back inside the drinking den.

'That's the sort of thing we are up against,' grumbled the third man. A tall lanky dude with more hair gracing his upper lip than his head, Nathan Clover was the bank manager. 'I don't envy you the task, sir.'

The new marshal's hands purposefully shifted to the pair of .36 Colt Navy pistols housed in a twin rigged gun belt mounted in the cross-draw manner. Wild Bill had always placed his trust in the reliable handguns, so Cal Bonner had followed suit. Thus far he had found no reason to doubt his old boss's choice. Only the crossover method of drawing distinguished the two law officers.

'I'll give the place a look over before I decide how best to tackle things,' he drawled out casually. 'No sense blundering in before I have gotten a feel for what's needed.'

A questioning regard panned across the three hovering officials.

'Anything you want, just let us know,' the mayor declared. 'I have taken the opportunity of booking you in with a widow lady, Marge Gillett. She runs the best rooming house in town. You should be comfortable there.'

Cal gave a satisfied nod of approval. 'Much obliged. I take it the job includes board and lodging?'

It didn't. But Doc Bailey quickly stepped in before the mayor could challenge the contention. 'Of course, sir. All part of the deal.'

Mayor Wishart deigned it prudent to curb the disparity hovering on his lips.

'I'll bid you good day then, gentlemen,' the new town marshal said, picking up his valise and sauntering off down the middle of Kingman Street.

'What do you reckon, Henry?' Clover asked. 'Has he gotten the makings?'

'We can only hope the extra we're paying for his services will be money well spent,' averred the prudent official. 'Only time will tell.'

Before he had even finished speaking, a group of newly arrived rannies galloped past. The three officials watched open-mouthed. In town for less than ten minutes and the guy was already being put to the test. The wild crew bore down on the unsuspecting new lawman.

'Out the way, mister, if'n you don't want to end up in the dirt,' the leader of the bunch hollered out as the six riders deliberately brushed past as near as damn it without touching the startled pedestrian. After all, these guys were expert horsemen. They did, however, manage to spatter his trousers with mud. It was all part of the fun.

'Looks like that fella could use a bath,' a young jigger honked out, much to the delight of his buddies.

The incident was quickly forgotten as they hurtled by, dragging their tough mustangs to a halt outside the Troubadour saloon where far more alluring entertainment was available. One cowpoke let off a pistol to announce their arrival as the brash dewlaps entered the premises to the accompaniment of jingle bob spurred boots.

Cal's narrowed gaze followed the rowdy bunch into the saloon. A thin yet frosty smile creased the craggy profile. 'Now I know where my first job lies,' he muttered to himself. 'But first I need to change my pants and fill up with a good meal at the Widow Gillett's.'

Wishart and his associates nervously watched as their new man carried on down the street. They all fervently dispatched silent entreaties upstairs that they had made the right decision. As Mayor Wishart had said, only time would tell.

Following the directions given to him, Cal hung a right down a side road beside the saddlery. And there it was on the far side at the end. The landlady was welcoming and made a fuss of her new guest. The burgeoning reputation of Bear River Cal Bonner had gone before him.

'We sure could do with a good lawman of your calibre here in Wichita.' Widow Gillett was a well-padded lady of middle years with white hair tied up in a large bun. But most important as far as the new guest was concerned, she knew her way around a kitchen.

'Those Texans spend a heap of dough,' she espoused firmly while dishing out the grub. 'And the young varmints want to have a good time. I don't begrudge them that. Trouble is they just don't know when to call it a day. All of them carry guns. Any guy hawking a hogleg around is likely to use it, especially when he's liquored up. We've had too many burials in the cemetery of late. It's to be hoped you can put a stop to it, Marshal.'

'I'll certainly do my best, ma'am. You can be sure of that,' Cal replied between mouthfuls of the best steak pie he had ever tasted. What the good widow said certainly made sense. He would keep it in mind. 'This sure is good cooking. Reckon I'm gonna enjoy it around here.'

Clad in fresh duds, his tooled leather gun rig strapped around his waist, the new lawman set off to make his mark on the town. And it wasn't long in coming.

The Troubadour was one of many such dens of vice fronting Kingman Street. He stepped inside. The noise hit him like a slap in the face. A piano was hammering away over to the right opposite the long mahogany bar. Some guys were dancing a jig with gaudily clad saloon girls, all eager to part the cowboys from their money. Around the edge gamblers plied their trade at circular green baize tables.

Straw on the floor soaked up spilled beer, not to mention sickly vomit. And judging by the sour reek it clearly hadn't been changed recently. The smell of these places always made Cal's nose wrinkle. A blend of stale beer, tobacco and unwashed bodies. Smoke from numerous quirlies mingled with that from tallow lamps. Even during daylight hours, saloons were dimly lit. A thick fug hung in the air.

Cal peered around. He was not averse to a drink. But in more congenial surroundings than this. His sharp eyes probed the hazy scene, all too soon settling on the cowpoke who had laughed in his face out on the street earlier. He was at the back waving a pistol around. With casual indifference the guy known as the Brazos Kid let off a couple of shots at some pot dogs resting on a shelf. Neither hit their target. He was too full of liquor to shoot straight.

A flinty gleam was reflected in the new marshal's gaze as he advanced down the room. The majority paid him no heed, being too intent on their own pleasures. Some who were more observant paused on spotting the shiny badge pinned to the guy's leather vest. Only when he was no more than three feet from the culprit did the cowpoke heed his presence.

'Well if'n it ain't that poor sap who nearly caused my horse to bolt,' Brazos slurred. 'What you doing in here, mister? Well past your bedtime, I'd say.' The guy was so drunk he hadn't even noticed the revered star.

'You tell him, Brazos,' echoed one of his buddies.

Cal fastened a warning gaze onto the cocky braggart. 'I'll take that gun, fella,' he voiced in a low yet meaningful utterance. 'Reckon it's a mite too dangerous for a wet-nosed kid like you to be toting around.' He held out his hand.

Brazos growled. Suddenly this was no jovial piece of banter. 'And who the hell are you to order me around, buster?'

Cal tapped his chest. 'I'm the new marshal. And you're disturbing the peace. Now I'd be obliged for that peashooter.'

'You want it? Then come take it. That is if'n you've gotten the nerve,' was the snarled response. The gun swung towards the menacing presence.

Without uttering any further warnings, the marshal quickly stepped forward and let rip a punishing right fist that slammed into the exposed jaw. The Kid never saw it coming. His head snapped back, blood pouring from a split lip. Before he slumped to the ground, Cal grabbed the falling body and slung it over his shoulder. Only then did he realize that his retreat had been cut off by the Kid's pals.

'Hey, fella, you can't do that,'

shouted one, brandishing his own hogleg.

'I just did, now step aside or you'll be joining this lump of dog dirt in the hoosegow.' With bold aplomb, Bear River Cal stamped down the full length of the saloon towards the hunched figures of the Texan cowboys. His left arm supported the limp body; his right held one of the Navy Colts. 'I ain't funning, boys. One false move and death comes a-calling.'

The marshal's audacious manner caused the young punks to hold back, uncertain of their response. Such bald-faced affrontery was something they had never previously encountered. The cowboys knew that any retaliation on their part in the form of gunplay could be curtains for the Brazos Kid, whose inert form was protecting the lawman's back. A purposeful yet measured tread echoed on the floorboards as men quickly stepped aside to let the marshal pass.

Before leaving the Troubadour, Cal

turned round to address the now silent crowd. 'As of tomorrow, the wearing of guns within the town limits is banned. Hand your rigs to the bartender and collect them when you leave town.'

A brief pause followed allowing the patrons to digest this momentous declaration. Guys looked at one another in astonishment, unsure they had heard right. Buckling on your shooting iron was as much a part of a guy's daily routine as stepping into his trousers. Every cowboy felt naked without one.

'You can pick this jigger up in the morning for a fine of ten dollars,' the marshal declared now that he had their full attention. 'And there'll be another ten charged for laundering those pants of mine you messed up earlier. The name's Cal Bonner. Some folks call me Bear River. Remember it if'n you decide to cause any more trouble in Wichita. Cos I'm here to stay.'

And with that parting shot he was gone. For a full minute, no words were uttered. Then a surge of noise erupted as men eagerly tossed views around regarding the recent incident. The bulldogging of the Brazos Kid in the Troubadour spread around town with the speed of a rampant prairie fire. Only one day into the job, and already Cal had made his presence felt in no uncertain terms.

The name of Bear River Cal Bonner was on everybody's lips. Some were more than pleased to have a tough enforcer to curb the excesses that had threatened to overrun the town. Others, however, were less than eager to add their support. Cody Meek was one such guy. Arrows of hatred bore into the tinstar's back as he sauntered off back to the jailhouse.

2

A Surprise for Browny

That had been six months before.

Cal stirred. Some kind of noise had interrupted the delightful slumber. He shook off the unwanted disturbance and turned over. The blankets were pulled over his head so as to resurrect the dreamy image of the enticing Candy Flowers.

A loud hammering on the outside door of the jail-house jerked the marshal from his sweet deliberations. Always a light sleeper — in this job it was an essential prerequisite — he was instantly awake. His pair of Navy Colts dangled from a hook beside the cot. He grabbed one and was on his feet in an instant. Although a weak sun was just about peeping through the window blinds, it was still far too early for social calls.

Had those darned cowpokes decided on an early raid to free their incarcerated buddies? That was his first thought. Their leader, the ramrod called Wyoming Bill, had laid down a warning that no hick tinstar was going to hold any of his boys. Cal had ignored the idle threat regarding it as nothing more than drink talk. Those fellas had been at the hard stuff all the previous night. They ought to have been sleeping it off at this hour.

Another blow rattled the door frame. This time it was accompanied by a panic-stricken cry. 'You in there, Marshal?' The crackling voice was that of Nightjar, the ostler from the livery stable who only seemed to come alive after dark. 'Let me in quick. I have something important to tell you.'

Bonner opened the door and let the guy in. 'What's this all about?' he said rubbing the grit from his eyes.

'There's a jasper down at the stable been asking after you,' Nightjar blurted out. 'And he sure didn't look the friendly sort. A troublemaker if'n you ask me. I'd say he had Mex blood in him mixed with a dose of Indian. A real shifty character.'

'So did this guy have a name?'

Nightjar paused to draw breath. He had clearly run all the way from the bottom end of town. 'Any chance of a snort, Marshal?' he enquired hopefully. Doleful eyes leaned towards the half empty bottle of whiskey on the lawman's desk. 'Just to clear my head you understand.'

Bonner's response was a wry smirk. 'Help yourself.'

The livery man imbibed a hefty swig, breathed out a sigh of delight, and sat down on the marshal's cot. 'The guy looked like he'd ridden a long way. His horse was all lathered up and covered in dust. But that pistol on his hip was well-oiled. It sure didn't look like it was there for show.'

'The name, Nightjar. That's what I need to know.'

'Calls himself Browny Jagus. Queer name for a half-breed,' replied the ostler taking another snort before hurrying on, 'but I said you had been called out of town on business and wouldn't be back until later in the day. Did I do right, Marshal?'

'Browny Jagus,' Bonner muttered under his breath. 'So you've showed up after all this time.' The lawman's eyes misted over as he recalled the last time he had set eyes on the gunman.

That had been when he had been marshal of Crested Butte. Jagus had been caught cheating in a faro game. He had pulled a gun and threatened to shoot the dealer. It was a piece of skulduggery intended to shift the blame away from Jagus himself. Only Cal's swift use of his meaty fists had prevented a murder charge being laid at the braggart's door. Such was the intense furore among the regular patrons, that Jagus was made to suffer the indignity of being tarred and feathered, then run out of town on a rail. He had sworn to get even with the man he blamed for his humiliation.

That was not the last he had heard of the killer. Jagus had gone on to become a noted gunslinger said to have nine notches carved on his gun butts. He clearly had Bear River Cal in mind to make it into double figures and earn himself a solid reputation at the same time. So here he was in Wichita. At least it saved Cal the trouble of going in search of the lamebrain.

'You all right, Marshal? Looks like some ghost just walked over your grave,' muttered the anxious ostler.

'Just some guy I had dealings with in a past life, is all. You sure did the right thing telling me, Nightjar,' the lawman praised the ostler, 'but keep it under your hat. We don't want the good citizens of Wichita getting themselves in a lather knowing that a guy like Jagus is in their midst.'

'You got my word on it,' the old guy promised. 'Watch your step though, Marshal, that skunk has a reputation for catching his marks unawares. I heard he ain't averse to backshooting if'n the chance arises.'

'Much obliged for the advice, old timer,' Cal acknowledged with a nod, even though he knew all about the sneaky tricks pulled by Browny Jagus. 'I sure will keep a sharp lookout.' Cal called the ostler back as he was about to leave. 'If'n you see him skulking around, you could drop the hint that I got back earlier than planned and he'll find me at the barber's shop when it opens at nine o'clock. Meanwhile I have me a dream to catch up on.'

And with that he settled down, the wistful smile once again suffusing his features.

He and Candy Flowers had been walking out for the last month. They had become kind of close and Cal was hoping to invite her to the theatre this coming Saturday. There was a travelling show arriving direct from Abilene with an 'internationally renowned sensation' topping the bill. Advertisements had been plastered all over town. It wasn't often that such high-quality entertainment was on offer in a cow town like Wichita. It promised to be a well-attended event. So Cal would need to buy tickets soon before they ran out. How to ask the lady in question if she would accompany him had been taxing his thoughts all week.

But first there was the matter of dealing with Browny Jagus.

Cal was in no hurry. Let the guy think he had the upper hand. It would make him careless and give Cal the break he needed to take him down. After an early breakfast in Polly Jayne's Pancake Parlour, he was walking down the boardwalk past the entrance to the Prairie Dog saloon when the proprietor stepped outside. 'Howdy there, Marshal,' Cody Meek proclaimed with breezy good nature that failed to reach the flinty gaze. 'You seem in a bit of a hurry.'

'Just minding my own business, Cody,' came back the caustic retort.

These two men were not best buddies. 'You should try it sometime.'

The saloon owner ignored the jibe. 'I hear that Browny Jagus is on the prod. Word's out that the betting shop is offering six to four odds he takes you out. But I ain't so sure. Reckon a smart guy like you will come out the winner. So I'm backing you, Marshal. Don't disappoint me. I'm a poor loser.' The malignant smirk was lost on the lawman who had walked on past.

'I'm touched by your faith in me, Cody.' The marshal's reply was chock full of disdain. 'I'll do my best to help fill your pockets. It'll make up for the extra rental I hear the town council is recommending.'

Meek sneered at the disappearing back. 'I'll get you one day, mister,' he mumbled to himself. 'That's a promise. And I'll even pay for your tombstone.'

The clock was striking the ninth hour of the new day when the marshal entered Clipper Jim's barbering emporium. The variety of aromas that filled the small room were in stark contrast to those imbibed in the saloons. The man himself was sharpening his razor on a leather strop. A fussy little dude with red suspenders over a white shirt, Jim Wicket fixed a wide eye onto his first customer. 'Surprised to see you in here so early, Marshal,' he declared, indicating for Cal to take the only seat.

'I have some unfinished business that needs settling,' the newcomer said without any elaboration. 'A guy always has the edge when he's smart, don't you think?'

'Couldn't agree more,' enthused the little guy. 'A smart fella always catches the early bird.' Wicket scratched his bald pate. 'Or something like that.'

Cal laughed as he unbuckled his rig and hung it on a hook. 'Guess that has to be me then.' He sat down allowing Clipper to sling a white cloth over him. 'Mind if'n I face the door while you do the business?' he added.

Jim gave the unusual request a puzzled frown. Most guys like to see what's happening on top through the mirror. But as they say, the customer is always right. So he swung the chair around on its pivot as requested, making no comment.

'What's it to be then, Marshal? Hair cut and shave?' asked the barber getting down to business. 'I have some fine new hair lotion just arrived from Kansas City. Rumour has it the gals go crazy over a fella wearing this stuff.' He held the bottle to Cal's nose. 'What do you reckon?'

'Smells a mite too tarty for me. I'll stick with my usual.'

'Please yourself,' came back the rather miffed response.

Cal settled back while the barber slapped lather on his face. Jim took up the sharpened razor and began the delicate process of stubble removal. No more than halfway through, his hand began to tremble.

'Some'n bothering you, Clipper?' Cal

asked. His eyes were closed while he enjoyed the barber's expert ministrations. But his mind was wholly focused on what he knew was about to happen.

'Th-there's a g-guy just c-come in and h-he's pointing a g-g-g . . . ' That was as far as the stuttered warning got before a shot rang out. The sharp report blasted off the walls of the enclosed space, startling a lazy cat occupying the window ledge. It shot out the open door.

But the gunshot had not originated from the Remington clutched in Browny Jagus's right hand. The outlaw thought he had the marshal at his mercy. He had watched from the far side of the street as Bonner had strolled down to Clipper Jim's. The leery grin on his ugly mush pointed to this particular gun-down being a piece of cake. The marshal's gunbelt hanging up out of reach gave Jagus the false assumption that his victim was unarmed.

But Cal Bonner knew exactly how

the shifty mind of this varmint operated, and he was ready. Calling a guy out for a one-to-one showdown was not his style. Too dangerous by far.

So the wily town tamer adopted similar tactics. When the underhanded critter made his move, Cal knew the barber would splutter out a garbled warning. Although truth be told, the guy's sour reek gave him away. Browny was not known for his bodily hygiene. Cal's eyes remained firmly closed when the danger arrived. The hidden gun bucked in his hand beneath the white sheet. Jagus clutched at his shoulder and staggered back into the street. Total surprise at this unexpected outcome was written across the brutish contours.

The intended victim threw aside the barber's cloth, which now had a charred hole in the middle. Beneath was a small .41 calibre Deringer almost hidden in the meaty fist. Smoke dribbled from the single-shot weapon. Tiny compared to the Navy Colts, it could still pack a lethal punch at close quarters.

The bullet disabling the failed killer was not a killing shot. Jagus would survive to stand trial. Cal grabbed one of the Colts to cover the sneaky rat. A crowd had quickly gathered outside Clipper Jim's. Shooting in Wichita was still common enough when cowpokes first hit town and from those who chose to ignore the no-gun ruling. But never this early in the day.

'Played you at your own game, Browny. It's lucky for you I had my eyes closed else you've have been worm food by now. On your feet, buster. I have a nice itchy cell ready and waiting for a conniving rat like you. Now shift your ass.'

The marshal and his groaning prisoner shambled off up Kingman towards the jailhouse followed by the muttering crowd. 'One of you fellas go bring Doc Bailey to the hoosegow. I don't want this jasper bleeding to death afore he gets to stand trial.'

'Much obliged for that, Marshal,' Meek said, lighting up a cigar. 'You sure know how to look after yourself. And this town as well.' The compliment was double-edged with more than a hint of mordancy.

The lawman was not taken in. 'And don't you forget it,' he growled out. Then in a lighter vein declared to the crowd, 'Mr Meek here has just pocketed a heap of dough after backing the winner of this fracas. And I heard him promise that all drinks were on the house if'n he won the bet. That right, Cody?'

The smile on Meek's face slipped being replaced by a scowl colder than a mountain stream. His fists clenched. He would dearly have loved to stuff those words down Cal Bonner's throat. But he could not deny it now. That would be bad for business. He had been given no option other than to accede to the marshal's blatant falsehood.

Cal's smile matched that of the saloon owner for frostiness. The two adversaries held each other's gaze. But it was Meek who broke the mould first. 'That's right, folks. Honest Cody Meek never welches on a deal. You're all welcome at the Prairie Dog.' Roars of approval greeted the announcement. Free drinks were a rare occurrence in Wichita. A surge of early drinkers hurried across the street anxious to stake their claim just in case it all proved to be a chimera.

'One up to you, Bonner,' the saloon owner snarled out, though in a low voice so nobody else could hear. 'But you best watch your back. Browny Jagus was nought but an incompetent asshole. Didn't know one end of a gun from the other. But others will likely turn up who can finish the job properly.'

'You threatening me, Cody?' the marshal hissed, taking a step forward.

'Take it any way you want, mister.' Meek stood his ground drawing hard on the cigar. 'Tough guys like you always end up on Boot Hill.' He paused, delivering a sneering grimace. 'One way or another.'

Tight-lipped, Cal held himself in check. No purpose would be served rising to the varmint's bait. He was given no further time to consider the saloon johnny's waspish retorts. A cloud of dust from the far end of Kingman heralded the arrival of the weekly stage from Abilene. It was always a welcome diversion for everybody. The town marshal was no different. But he especially liked to check out new arrivals and apprise any suspicious characters of the no-guns ruling.

The team of six was wrestled to a thundering halt by a grey-bearded old muleskinner called Cannonball Coolidge. He was supported up top by a much younger guy, clutching a shotgun.

Along with a host of other curious residents, Cal wandered across to the Butterfield depot. Cody Meek speared his back with an odious look that spoke of dire tidings should the chance ever arise. He lit up another cigar and drew hard to assuage a mutinous inner turmoil. Another man joined him. One who was similarly ill-disposed towards the town's stringent lawman.

3

Unexpected Arrival

'That guy is becoming a thorn in our side, Cody,' the owner of the Crystal Chandelier Theatre remarked, sidling up to his business colleague. Perry Blaine was a suave well-dressed dude considering himself debonair and stylish as behove a true showman. The waxed moustache twitched. 'What are we going to do about him? I was hoping that Browny Jagus would provide the answer.'

Meek scoffed at his partner's apparent naïvety. 'That clown couldn't find his way out of a paper bag. What we need is a real gunslinger to finish the job.'

'He's only one man,' retorted Blaine scornfully. 'Surely we don't need to pay out big bucks to pack away one hick starpacker into his coffin.'

'That guy ain't no ordinary tinstar,' Meek iterated with some degree of inverted respect. A heavy-lidded gaze followed the lawman across the street. 'He's already cleared up boom towns in Colorado before joining Wild Bill in Abilene. The guy has eyes in the back of his head. How else d'you reckon he's survived for so long? Jagus found that out too late. And not only that. Bonner has solid back-up in the form of the mayor and Doc Bailey, plus others who don't relish a wide-open town.'

'Damned turncoats!' his colleague railed, adding his own mercenary reasons for getting rid of the town tamer. 'They sure as hell like the dough all these wild cowpokes bring in. But they can't take the hard graft guys like me and you put in to line their pockets. Critters like that make my skin crawl. Look over yonder.' Blaine aimed a finger to the burgeoning spread of Delano on the far side of the Arkansas River. 'Six months ago that dump was nought but a trading post. Now there's a couple of saloons plus a hen house, and more being erected as we speak. That trade should be over here.'

Delano was outside the jurisdiction of a town marshal, free country, and therefore not subject to the restrictions imposed by Cal Bonner. The saloons were open twenty-four hours a day, and guns were constantly being loosed off. The rising line of bluffs behind the row of hurriedly erected shacks made the unkempt amalgam totally unsuitable for expansion, although it was ideal for the rip-roaring antics of well-heeled drovers while the boom lasted.

Wichita on the other hand had prospered on the opposite side of the river. In addition to unlimited prairie grassland for the town to develop, herds brought up the trail from Texas did not have to brave the swirling waters of the Arkansas. In the rainy season, the river could become a raging torrent. So a bridge had been erected for people and horses to cross, but that was all.

Perhaps now the railroad had arrived a more permanent structure would be built.

Meek nodded glumly. 'You're right, Perry. More and more of these drovers are heading across the river. It's bad for business. Something has to be done. And soon.'

'I reckon that I might have the answer to our problem,' Blaine declared in a secretive manner. A be-ringed hand caressed his smooth chin.

The saloon boss threw a hopeful glance at his associate. Anything to halt the vice-like grip Cal Bonner was throwing around their lucrative enterprises was worth listening to. 'You gonna fill me in then?'

'Better leave it until later. I need to meet the stage,' Blaine replied, setting his hat straight and adjusting his necktie.

His partner gave the comment a puzzled frown. 'What's wrong with now?'

'Remember that gal I was telling you

about, the one I met in Kansas City?'

'You mean Tilly Dumont, the singer?'

Blaine nodded. 'Well I've booked her in for a couple of weeks at the Chandelier. And she comes complete with a troupe of dancing girls as well. They're following later today on a wagon along with their costumes and props.' This eye-opening revelation was complemented by a sleazy leer. 'I'm sure you'll find one of them compliant enough to satisfy even your lurid appetite.'

'What in blue blazes do you mean by that?' The saloon owner's angular features visibly coloured while he protested forcefully. But Blaine was already making his way across the street.

The stagecoach was surrounded by a host of eager spectators. Its arrival always caused the same pandemonium. Apart from cowpunchers and cattle buyers, Wichita received few other visitors. Any stranger was avidly questioned before being allowed to go about his business. The only female passengers were usually those seeking work in the saloons or other more earthy places of entertainment.

'Any trouble, Cannonball?' the Butterfield agent asked the crusty old timer sitting on the bench seat up front.

'Nary a thing except for a few wandering Kiowas who gave us the once over,' replied the hardy stage driver. 'Young Butcher here scared 'em off when they took sight of the scatter gun he was toting.' He then passed down a leather satchel of mail while Yoke Butcher saw to the disembarkation of the passengers.

The first person to step down was a small bustling dude in a natty check suit. Harlem Mordecay briskly called for order to allow his protègè to alight.

And that was when a collective gasp from the assembled gathering called a halt to the babbling. The lady in question was dressed in a stylish manner that was clearly not that of the soiled dove variety. The neat hat complete with flamboyant ostrich plume sat atop a coiffure of elegant russet curls. With nonchalant aplomb, she accepted the hand of young Butcher while stepping down onto the boardwalk. The elegance of her posture caused men's eyes to pop, their tongues to hang out. This dame was definitely no common saloon moll.

'Make way if you please, gentlemen, to allow the lady some room,' warbled Mordecay ineffectually, trying to make a passage for his charge. 'We can't have an international singing star being jostled by riff-raff.'

The insult was lost as the multitude of excited onlookers fought to lay their peepers on the mysterious celebrity. That was when Perry Blaine chose to step forward.

'Pardon me, Mr Mordecay.' The rich baritone timbre drowned out the chaperone's shrill squawk as the theatre owner took control by raising his hands. A silence quickly ensued. 'Folks, may I present Miss Tilly Dumont, sensational star of the stage. Tilly has generously given her time to entertain us here in Wichita. And I'm sure you will all make her welcome. Tickets are on sale from midday.'

A roar went up from the crowd. Blaine raised a hand for silence as he took hold of the lady's hand. 'And one more thing. Miss Dumont has kindly agreed to be my wife.' Another resounding shout of approval greeted this surprise announcement. A wedding meant free drinks and plenty of grub.

The alleged prospective bride was less than impressed. This was no less a shock for her as well. A sweeping eyebrow lifted in astonishment. Her mouth fell open. The acerbic look aimed at the gushing impresario was less than endearing, as was the hissed rejoinder that contained more venom than a sidewinder's bite. 'All I said was that I'd think about it. That's the third time you've asked, Perry. Now give it a rest. You'll have an answer in my own good time.'

Blaine's smile remained pasted onto his sanguine features. He was nothing if not persistent. But like an irritating itch, to the lady in question such pushiness could rapidly become irksome. 'You can't blame a guy for trying, Tilly. And I'll keep on until you give me the right answer.' He was about to usher the singer inside the Crystal Chandelier when Cal Bonner stepped forward.

'Aren't you going to introduce me, Perry?' the marshal asked, doffing his hat. 'It isn't everyday that a lowly town marshal gets to meet such a grand celebrity.'

Blaine huffed, then with some degree of reservation did the honours.

Cal's head bowed curtly. But the icy gleam in his eyes failed to match the welcoming smile. Seeing his estranged wife arriving in Wichita after all this time was a startling revelation that had momentarily left him bereft of any kind of response. Then to hear she was romantically involved with the theatre owner had struck him like a sock to the jaw.

The couple had married while Cal was working the Colorado gold mining camp of Crested Butte. That had been five years before. His new bride had hoped that once the rough and ready berg was tamed, Cal would hang up his guns and settle down to a more prosaic way of life that was infinitely safer. Too many women have naïvely thought the same thing where their men folk were concerned. But a leopard never changes its spots.

What she hadn't counted on was the fact that a dull life tending store, or maybe growing crops on a farm, was anathema to Bear River Cal. He had been well and truly bitten by the adrenalin-pumping bug of excitement that maintaining the law offered. Settling down to a humdrum life was not for him. Other boom towns had followed until one day, Adele Bonner — as she was then called — had walked out.

When Cal returned home after running down a bunch of claim jumpers, a note was waiting for him on the kitchen table of their home in Bonanza. The 'Dear John' missive gave no indication as to where she had gone. All efforts to track her down led to dead ends. His wife clearly had no wish to be found.

At the time, Cal had been devastated. But time as the saying proclaims is the great healer. Yet here she now was in Wichita. In the intervening years Adele Bonner had clearly done very well for herself. And judging by the overtures being made by Perry Blaine, their own marriage meant nothing to her.

The theatre owner's breezy introduction went over the marshal's head. 'You did say the name was Tilly Dumont?' he asked with barely concealed disdain.

'A stage name, Marshal,' the woman breathed out in a low voice after eyeballing her husband. With great difficulty, she somehow managed to maintain a cool front. Tilly did not appear to have been caught off guard by the unexpected meeting in the same way as her husband. It was almost as if she had expected the encounter. That said, his sudden appearance after all these years still left her flummoxed. Swallowing down her bewilderment, Tilly eventually recovered her poise. 'A girl has to have some privacy. It seems like I've heard about a tough lawman by the name of Bonner who once lived in Bonanza. That wouldn't happen to be you would it, Marshal?'

'A man has to earn a living, ma'am,' her estranged husband replied flatly. 'Maybe if people understood that upholding the law is vital for everybody's safety and well-being, they might have more respect for those who choose to wear the badge of office.' He tapped his chest meaningfully.

'And perhaps those same men might have the tact to pay more attention to the feelings of those who support them.'

'It doesn't always end up that way, does it Miss . . . Dumont?'

Blaine was becoming edgy. He didn't cotton to the marshal commandeering the attention of his future intended. The hidden agenda being batted back and forth went over his head. 'Time you were settling in, Tilly,' he snapped out acidly. 'I'm sure it's been a tiring ride from Abilene. You understand, don't you Marshal?' He took the woman's arm to lead her away.

Tilly shook him off; penetrating eyes were still fixed onto the stolid badge-toter. 'From what I've heard, most lawman have very little appreciation of how a woman's mind works. The job, it appears, surpasses everything else. Even those they claim to hold dear.' Tilly turned away to hide her evident distress. Setting eyes on the man she had once loved had resurrected emotions she had long thought dead and buried. 'I am sure that Marshal Bonner is no different from all the others of his kind.'

Moments later she was gone.

Adele Bonner was now a very

different woman from the one Cal had married all those years ago. She had even changed her name and profession. It was a mighty leap up the social ladder. From a humble school teacher, she had attained the dizzy heights as a grandiose singing sensation held in adulation by the masses.

He on the other hand was but little changed. Perhaps it would be as well if they made the final break. A divorce seemed the only viable option. Then they could both move on. But did he really want such a terminal ending?

Cal wandered away. His mind was in a total quandary. There was much to think on. The crowd dispersed, totally unaware of the poignant exchange between the two people. But there was one person who clearly suspected that all was not as it appeared on the surface.

Candy Flowers was standing on the veranda above the crowd. From her elevated position she had witnessed the tears in the celebrity's eyes, the pain and heartache that the meeting had caused. The fixed smile on the singer's face was a sham. A formulaic greeting expressly for the masses. But Candy was not fooled. Only a woman could have picked up on the inner torment emanating from another.

It was obvious to the croupier that these two people had a shared past. And it was patently one of the heart. Although what exactly that entailed was not as yet clear.

Candy was determined, however, to find out.

If this woman had designs on her man, she would fight tooth and nail to foil any liaison. No matter what the outcome. She might be a modest girl hailing from the wrong side of the tracks, but Candy Flowers had her pride. Nobody was going to get the better of her.

4

Hell Hath No Fury . . .

With conflicting thoughts of his alienated wife occupying every waking moment, Cal forgot to book tickets for the forthcoming performance at the Crystal Chandelier. As such, by the time he was reminded of the promised liaison by Candy, every seat had been taken. Such was Tilly Dumont's renown that her entire booking had been a sell-out within hours of the ticket office opening.

It was accordingly a thoroughly downbeat Cal Bonner who had to relay the unfortunate tidings to his lady friend. She received the news with lukewarm indifference. Yet inside she was seething. Candy was well aware that her beau's mind had been elsewhere in recent days. And now she knew the reason why.

'I sure am sorry about that, Candy. But I'll make it up to you,' bleated the abashed lawman after breaking the unwholesome news. 'Perhaps we can go to the Palace Hotel for a meal tonight. They serve the best grub in town, all high class stuff prepared by a French chef.' Cal twiddled with his hat hopefully. 'So what do you say? Is it a date?'

But Candy was having none of it. 'It most certainly is not, Marshal.' Her narrow shoulders lifted. An imperious cock of the head indicated her derision for the tardy offer. 'I'm working tonight, and will be for the foreseeable future as far as you're concerned.' And with that cutting remark, she stamped off wiggling her ample hips.

No man was going to make her a laughing stock. Perhaps in a day or two, she would forgive him. After all, Cal Bonner was a good catch. Tall, handsome and daring, he was all that a single girl could wish for in a man. Her nose twitched. But he needed to see that Candy Flowers was no pushover.

She knew he was watching as she crossed over Kingman. But the girl maintained a straight course without turning round before entering the Prairie Dog where she had risen to the prestigious position of chief croupier.

Cal slunk away. Being tossed aside by two women in a week was bad for his reputation.

When he returned to the jailhouse to reluctantly finish off some paperwork, Cal was surprised to see an envelope had been pushed under the door. He frowned, wondering what it could contain. Only one way to find out. A shock awaited him. Inside was a ticket to the opening performance of the *Showcase Extravaganza* featuring legendary songbird Tilly Dumont.

Cal was dumbfounded. But the ticket was only for one seat. Who could have sent it? Only two people had access to those extra tickets reserved for special guests. And he was darned certain

Perry Blaine would not desire his presence at the Chandelier. His heart fluttered at the notion that perhaps there was a chance for him after all.

Was this his opportunity to show Adele that he had changed? The old two-fisted sharp-shooting Cal Bonner had matured. Perhaps he could even be persuaded to adopt a more common-place lifestyle. But would that now be enough for a famous stage celebrity?

He quickly hurried back to his lodging house to remove his best suit from the closet where it had hung ignored for too long. It was a mite creased and dusty. Marge Gillett would be able to tidy it up once she learned what had happened. The widow was a romantic at heart and would have all kinds of advice to bestow. All of which would float over Cal's head. He knew exactly what he had to do if'n he was to win back the hand of his only true love.

'You must be going somewhere special tonight, Cal,' the kindly woman enquired, setting his dinner on the table. 'May I say how handsome you look. And a close shave no less as well. That Candy Flowers is a lucky girl.'

'Me and Candy ain't exactly on speaking terms at the moment.'

'That's a shame. I thought you two were getting on so well,' Marge sighed, pouring out a cup of coffee to go with the chicken casserole. 'It sure ain't my business to pry, but if'n you want to talk about it, I'm a good listener. And discreet too.'

'Guess we just weren't meant for each other.'

Cal had no wish to reveal his true intentions and hopes for the future. Things may or may not work out between him and Adele. But he intended to give it his best shot. And if'n that smarmy chiseller, Perry Blaine objected, he knew what to expect. Cal's fists gripped the knife and fork tighter. Marge Gillett left him alone to eat his meal. She could see that no revelations were to be divulged over the dining table.

* ★ ★

Cal was in his seat when the band struck up at seven o'clock precisely. They played a couple of lively tunes before the dancing girls came on to a rowdy collection of hoots and lewd comments. It was all part of the fun. He was surprised to find himself in the more privileged part of the theatre rather than the main auditorium containing the cheap seats. Those in this raised gallery were able to relax in comfortable padded chairs. Even the floor was carpeted.

More exclusive still were the closed-off boxes in which the town dignitaries and their wives were ensconced. He could see the mayor and Doc Bailey sitting together on one side. Switching his gaze to the far side invoked a twisted frown on seeing the preening face of Cody Meek and one of his hostesses.

Harlem Mordecay introduced each of the acts with a few risqué jokes thrown in to keep the rabble in the stalls entertained. To follow there were acrobats, jugglers and even a performing dog. The final act before the interval was given a special introduction.

The band played the opening bars of a song with which everybody in the room was familiar, 'Sweet Betsie From Pike'. The dulcet tones of the singer reverberated around the room. Then she appeared, sashaying on stage clad in a gorgeous outfit that left little to the imagination. The room erupted. This was what they had all come to see.

Cal stared at his wife, unable to remove his eyes. She was just as lovely as he remembered. Lust mingled with resentment at others being able to enjoy what he considered to be a private display. How could she have lowered herself to this? The innocent young school ma'am he had married was now public property, and it hurt.

More songs followed, but Cal barely heard a single word. Before the curtain fell to herald the end of the first half of the show, the marshal made his way down to the main auditorium. Passing through the adjacent room where gambling and refreshments were laid on for the dignitaries, Cal failed to noticed the croupier at the roulette wheel.

Unknown to the lawman, Candy Flowers had been loaned to the theatre just for this opening night. The girl certainly spotted her alienated beau and the fact that he was headed for the performers' dressing rooms at the rear of theatre.

'And I know exactly where you're going, fella,' she murmured under her breath. Without any further ado, Candy called for one of the other girls to replace her. 'Take over for me will you, Riva. I won't be long,' she said. 'Just need to powder my nose.' Then she left, cautiously trailing after the oblivious Cal Bonner.

At the end of a corridor, she paused. Cal had stopped at the door occupied by the star of the show. His knock was restrained, cautious. A nervous expectancy gripped his innards. Would Adele be pleased to see him? Throw herself into his arms? Or would it be a summons to the final reckoning, that irrevocable split? Conflicting visions of hope and despair tore at his heartstrings in the brief seconds it took for a muted response to come through the closed door.

'Come in.' The summons was brisk and upbeat. Tilly was still basking in the adulation from the crowd following her rousing performance on stage. That's what fame did and why she enjoyed it so much. The door opened. The lady in question sat facing a mirror rearranging her hair and make-up for the second half of the show. 'Take a seat,' she said oblivious to the identity of the visitor. 'I'll be with you in a second.' All her attention was focused on achieving the perfect image.

'Hello, Adele. It's been a long time.'

For a moment there was no reaction from the singer. Nobody had addressed her by her birth name since that last day in Bonanza when her husband had left their home to pursue yet more violent miscreants. She had become so used to being called Tilly. Then the penny dropped. Her heart beat faster. Her back stiffened. Slowly she turned round to face the man she had prayed would come.

And there he was. Neither spoke for a long minute. It was Adele who broke into the charged atmosphere. 'I was wondering if you'd come,' she whispered in that husky drawl that had so captivated him all those years ago. 'It seems strange to be called by my real name after all this time.'

'When you sent the theatre ticket, I figured that maybe . . . ' He swallowed. A dry tongue anxiously lapped across his lower lip. ' . . . Maybe there might possibly be a chance for us to..'

'That all depends on you, Cal,' the girl interrupted. 'I've never stopped loving you. Sure, there have been men who wanted more than I could give.

Perry Blaine is the latest and most irksome of the bunch. But there could never be anyone else.'

'I guess it's all up to me then,' the lawman declared advancing slowly into the room. 'Whether I can manage to forsake the life I lead.'

'If you love me as much as I love you, that has to be a consideration. I can't live with the constant danger of you being shot down like a dog. That was the reason I left in the first place.'

Cal reached out and took her hand in his. A tingling sensation rippled through his lean frame. 'I ain't never looked at another woman since you left. And that's a fact. It was always you, Adele. And still is.'

Her will to resist this man's earnest entreaties was wilting rapidly. Yet still there were doubts. 'I have made a good life for myself over the years. Fame and fortune is a potent inspiration. But that can't be all that life has to offer.'

Their eyes met. Then their bodies intertwined in that age-old ritual first enacted when Adam found Eve. At that moment, nothing else mattered.

Outside, Candy Flowers couldn't bear to hear anymore. The man she had so earnestly thought would carry her off on a white horse to live that fairytale dream was nought but a cheating rat. No better than all the other wheedling skunks in whom she had placed her trust.

Tears flowed. But they soon dried up as a seething demand for revenge burned deep in her bosom. Candy had not become a leading lady in a man's world without nerves of steel and a skin tougher than bull hide. Anybody who had ever messed with this dame had come out much the worse for their encounter. She toyed with the small pocket Wesson .22 pistol in her purse.

On more than one occasion Candy had been forced to use it, and to lethal effect. Tough guys who thought they could have it all were now worm bait.

There had been numerous other men in her life. All had promised the earth and ended up leaving her high and dry once their passion had been sated. Only Cal Bonner had seemed genuine, a true gentleman. Now even he had played her false.

Yet because her hopes had been raised to such a high level, equally her thirst for revenge was no less ardent. She stumbled back down the corridor. For the rest of the evening she was barely able to function.

She had later poured her heart out to Riva Speedwell, the other croupier. The girl had voiced her commiserations. 'Don't take it to heart, honey,' the older woman sympathized. 'All men are the same. Just one thing on their minds. My advice is to forget about him.'

But Candy was beyond that. She wanted revenge. And it showed. Mistakes were made; gamblers needed pacifying when their winnings were short-changed. A stream of virulent cussing issued from between those luscious pouting lips bringing startled looks from nearby punters. Candy was oblivious to the stares.

'What in tarnation is wrong with you tonight, Candy?' Blaine hollered after challenging her following the third such episode. 'You're normally a sharp operator on the tables. Now get a grip on yourself, or there'll be trouble.'

'Sorry about that, boss,' the girl profusely apologized, realizing that no good would come of allowing herself to fall apart. 'I received some bad news earlier. My mother passed away a couple of days ago.'

'I'm sorry to hear that,' the theatre owner said, curtailing his angry tirade. 'But you can't allow personal feelings to interfere with your work. Take an hour off to settle yourself down. Then go see about your ma's funeral. I'll square it with Meek.'

Candy thanked the guy then left to figure out how best to make that bastard pay for treating her like dirt. Back in her room later that night, she soon calmed down. Her thoughts moved swiftly towards retribution.

There was no way she would allow that slattern to steal her man. Candy had reconciled herself to the inevitable fact that she and the marshal were now history. So how to make certain her chilling thirst for vengeance achieved a satisfactory conclusion?

It was not until the quiet of the early hours that the idea was born. The skunk was going to learn at first hand that hell hath no fury like a woman scorned. Candy's eyes burned brighter than the silver-painted moon shining through her window. Marshal Cal Bonner had definitely bitten off more than he could chew. No man was going to toss her aside like an old shoe.

Candy had accrued savings of around 300 dollars. It had originally been to have a special wedding dress and trousseau made. Now that money was to hire the services of men who harboured a grudge against the Wichita lawman.

Wyoming Bill Gannon had stayed behind in town after his two men were thrown into the can. The foreman's threat to bust them out had come to nothing. Bear River Cal's fists had seen to that. The three men were feeling humiliated after being forced to pay their fines. And they had voiced their resentment in no uncertain terms in the Prairie Dog following their release from custody.

Although she had no liking for the raucous trio, Candy was sure that 300 bucks would be enough to persuade them to remove Cal Bonner from circulation, on a permanent basis. The cowboys were known to have established themselves in the Plainsman saloon. It was more than likely by this time that the dough they had made from the cattle drive would be almost spent. Any day now they would be forced to head back south to Texas.

She needed to act fast.

Next morning Candy hurried down to an abandoned shack on the edge of town, which the trio had appropriated. Smoke dribbled from the stovepipe telling her they were at home. If such could be said of the grubby hovel. Her nose wrinkled in distaste. The smell of stale sweat and rancid grease had even permeated the wooden shell. With some degree of hesitancy, she knocked on the door.

It opened slowly, a gun barrel poking through. 'Who's there?' posed the suspicious growl of Smiley Dodd. The cowpoke had earned his nickname after a knife-fight that went wrong. His opponent's unlucky slash had ripped a chunk from his lip giving the cowboy a permanent leer.

'It's me, Candy Flowers,' the girl croaked as the odious reek tried to escape the confines of its prison. 'I have a proposition for you boys.'

'Let her in,' hollered out the voice of Wyoming Bill. 'This might prove interesting.' Gannon was of a mind they were going to be offered a little fun on the side by the delectable croupier.

Candy recognized the lecherous crow and quickly put him right. 'This visit ain't for what you're thinking, Bill. So get that out of your dirty mind straight away.' No more time was wasted in idle chatter as the visitor got down to business. 'How would you boys like to earn 300 bucks?'

The startled cowpokes looked at one another. Divided between them that was more than three months' wages for a humble drover. 'What do we have to do for it?' Wyoming Bill shot back with a sceptical leer. 'Some punter vamoosed with the takings of your roulette wheel?' The three men chuckled.

Candy forced herself to ignore the caustic jibe. She needed lowlife skunks like these to retrieve her self-respect. She cast a jaundiced eye over the sour-smelling trio. Their duds were badly in need of repair. The only things about them kept in good condition were the guns openly on display. That at least was a positive sign.

'I want somebody removed from my life,' she murmured in a low voice. 'Permanently!'

That soon caught their attention. All three had killed men at some point in their lives. But it had only been Indians and greasers trying to steal cattle. And they didn't count. This was something else entirely. 'We need to talk this over,' Gannon informed the girl as the three men moved away to discuss the proposition.

Five minutes later they returned. 'Three hundred ain't much for killing a guy who's done us no hurt,' Gannon said. His two buddies nodded their agreement.

'It's all I have. So take it or leave it,' the girl snapped. Hands on hips, she stared them out. Candy had no intention of walking away without a deal. 'Before rejecting my offer you should know that the guy I want removing is Marshal Bonner.'

'Bonner!' Snake-Eyed Bob Jarman exclaimed rubbing the bruise on his head, an unwelcome present from the much-hated lawman. 'I'd deem it a pleasure to cut that varmint down to size. What about you, buddy?'

Smiley Dodd was of an equal mind. 'I'm with you, Snake. That critter has been strutting around like a peacock for too darned long.' Both men looked to Bill Gannon for the final say-so.

'This turkey must have done something awful bad to turn you into such a goddamned fireball, Candy,' Gannon said, hawking out a lusty chuckle.

'My reason for wanting that sonofabitch out of the way is no concern of your'n,' she snapped back. 'Now are you in or out? There are plenty more dudes around who'd welcome the job.'

The foreman was not to be rushed. He knew this was in the bag. Only drunks or those with enough reason to go up against Bonner would accept such a job. But a little play-acting gave a boost to his ego. He lit up a smoke as if considering the proposition. A long minute passed before he palmed a large .36 Remington Rider revolver and stroked the long barrel.

'Reckon you'll be needing a fresh coat of oil if'n there's work to be done.' The ugly grin that split open a grizzled face told its own story. 'So how do you want this done, Candy?' he posited, holding out a hand for the agreed fee.

'Any way you want to play it,' she replied, trying to contain her eagerness. 'Just so long as the rat is taken off the streets. What I can tell you is that he always takes a coffee with bartender Wishbone Adderley in the Drovers' House around ten o'clock every morning.'

Candy stood up and turned to leave. A hundred dollars in used notes was slapped down on the table. 'That's on account. You get the rest after the job's done.' She paused at the door of the grubby pit. 'There's one condition. No mention of me when you call him out. And once you've done it, get out of Wichita fast and don't look back. I never want to see your ugly kissers again.'

And with that parting retort, she left the hired gunmen alone to discuss their strategy.

5

. . . Like a Woman Scorned

Candy was watching the street from her room above the Prairie Dog. The tense atmosphere showed on the girl's drawn face. Her fingers were gripping the windowsill so tight the knuckles showed whiter than the driven snow. Four days had passed since her clandestine meeting with the Lazy K rannigans. This morning was the time agreed for the showdown.

The need to assuage her humiliation had wavered not a jot during that interim period. If anything it had festered and grown. Having to live in such close proximity to that pair of canoodling love rats made her skin crawl. Thick-rouged lips drawn back in a rictus of loathing revealed an irreparable determination to see this dire episode through to its brutal climax.

Moments later her hate-filled eyes glittered with anticipation. There they were. Three horses walking side-by-side up the middle of Kingman. Hats pulled low, the riders sat erect as they swung in to a hitching rail two blocks down from the Drovers' House. They slowly dismounted before checking their weapons. In line abreast, they walked down towards the diner, stopping outside. There, they spread out to present a wider target.

Wyoming Bill's gruff summons penetrated the closed window where Candy stood. 'You in there, Bonner?' It was a melodramatic question. Gannon had been fully apprised of the marshal's regular habit. 'I'm calling you out, tinstar. So don't keep me waiting.'

Passers-by stopped. At one time in the not too distant past, shoot-outs had been a regular occurrence in Wichita. But since the passage of the law that banned the wearing of guns on the streets, such incidents had been dramatically curtailed.

Again the hard, grating voice rang out. 'You hear me, Bonner? Are you coming out or do we have to come in and get you?'

Inside the diner, Cal was enjoying his usual coffee and a slice of cinnamon cake. Being thus interrupted was irksome. He scowled. Who in tarnation was causing a ruckus at this hour of the day? He turned to a young boy employed to clear the tables. 'Go on out there, kid, and see what this jasper wants. Disturbing my snack time ain't to be taken lightly.'

'Sure thing, Marshal,' the youngster replied, eager to add some excitement to his mundane life. Willy Juniper hurried outside where the men were waiting.

The three Texans had their slickers pulled back revealing well-kept hardware worn at the hip and ready for use. Broad-brimmed high-crowns shaded their upper features. Grim snarls told the kid this was no friendly visit.

Nerves clutched at the boy's guts. 'The m-marshal wants to know what you w-want with him,' he stammered out.

'You tell that son of the devil it's unfinished business with Wyoming Bill Gannon.'

Willy hustled back inside the diner. 'I heard him, kid,' Bonner said before the boy could open his mouth. He flicked a dime up into the air. The shiny coin was snatched out of the air with practiced dexterity, its validity tested with a quick bite. Satisfied, the dime vanished into Willy's pocket.

Cal grinned at the kid's distrustful action. He finished his coffee and stood up. 'You go tell those fellows that I'll be out when I've finished my cake.' Willy just stood there, transfixed. 'Go on, boy, earn your pay. We can't have those bad boys coming in here, can we?'

'N-no sir, w-we sure can't,' Willy replied, hurrying back to relay the marshal's response to the call out.

80

Gannon was fuming. 'What does that critter think he's a-doing of? Telling me to wait on his pleasure?' But the foreman had no wish to enter the diner where his adversary would have a distinct advantage.

'What we gonna do, Bill?' asked Smiley Dodd. 'We can't just hang around out here. It ain't dignified.'

The need for a decision was taken out of their hands, the object of their quest appearing from the side alley abutting the Drovers' House. Bonner had exited through the rear door to catch the three gunmen on the hop. Bonner had removed his jacket to reveal black pants held up by suspenders. The twin-rigged gun belt with its crossed revolvers was now all the easier to reach, a vital necessity when having to face down three mean-eyed skunks seeking revenge.

'You boys looking for me?' he said breezily, effecting a slight bow.

The three men had been caught wrong-footed. And they knew it.

Wyoming Bill was the first to recover. He swung to face the quarry pushing aside his flapping slicker to reveal the Remington Ryder. 'You know why we're here, Bonner. Nobody buffaloes my boys without a payback.'

'Damn right they don't,' iterated Jarman. 'I still got me the lump.'

These guys were on the prod and there was no stepping back now. Yet still the marshal hoped to steer things to a more peaceful solution. 'I don't know you fellas. What's your beef with me?'

'Don't try that on with us, mister,' Gannon snarled, clenching his eager fists. 'You gave these two guys sore heads then threw them in the pokey. I had to pay out good money for their release.'

'Cut this jawing, boys, and let's get to shooting,' Smiley Dodd interjected reaching for his holstered Manhattan. His pistol cleared leather and spat flame. But the shot was hurried. The kind of blunder made by an amateur gun wielder. One who was more used to shooting rabbits or driving off Indian raiders than facing down a guy of Bear River Cal's proficiency. It went wide, smashing a window to his right.

The tough marshal proved he was no slouch in that regard, and accordingly made the cowboy pay for his foolishness. Two bullets slammed into the guy's chest punching him back. Dodd was gagging on his own blood, coughing out a stream of red as he dropped to his knees.

The fight was well and truly on. Wyoming Bill drew next and got off two shots. One clipped the lawman's arm drawing blood, the other lifting his hat.

The foreman's eyes widened on realizing he had made the same error as his sidekick. He took a step back to correct his aim. Too late. Time had run out for the Lazy K ramrod. Cal smiled. 'You guys never learn. A snatched shot is worse than no shot at all.' His gun barked twice more. Bill Gannon spun around like a demented puppet, then reeled across the street clutching at a hitching post. His gun lifted, but the fatally injured man's strength was fast ebbing away. A third shot finished him off.

Cal ignored him as he swung to face Snake-Eyed Bob. 'One shot left, mister. Do you want it?'

The cowpoke's staring gaze focused on the barrel of the Navy Colt pointing his way. All the bluster of moments before had been dissipated by the harshly imminent reality of a meeting with the Grim Reaper. In the manner of a burst balloon, the fight fizzled out of him. The grim result of challenging the renowned town tamer lay splattered across the dusty street for all to see.

Desperation scored the fear-ravaged face as Jarman pleaded for his life. He threw down his gun, hands lifting skywards. 'That business Gannon was talking about, it weren't us who wanted you out the way. We were paid to . . . '

Cal waved the excuses aside. The plea for mercy had fallen on deaf ears.

'Cut the crap, mister. I don't want to hear it.'

The Navy rose to deliver a final goodbye. A white-knuckled finger tightened on the trigger. The continued existence of Snake-Eyed Bob Jarman hovered on the brink. Then slowly and deliberately the threatening gun hand was lowered. A calm deliberation replaced the high-bound tension of moments before. There had been enough killing for one day. And how could he even have considered shooting down an unarmed man in cold blood? Cal shook off the mesmeric compulsion to finish the job.

'You're lucky that I have some unfinished business of my own to take care of.' His thoughts had shifted to the reconciliation with his wife. 'Now grab your horse and light out of here, pronto. And if'n I see your ugly mug in Wichita again, you'll be joining these turkeys in hell.'

Snake Jarman heaved a grateful sigh of relief. In no time he had mounted up and was spurring off up the street.

Cal just stood there in the middle of Kingman, his gun hanging limp by his side. Onlookers watched from cover. Wichita had become a much more civilized place since the new marshal had instigated the no-arms ruling. So the gunning down of two cowboys, now with their life force darkening the ground, came as a startling reminder of how fragile the peace could be.

After calling for a couple of men to go fetch the undertaker, the marshal slumped off back to his office. He badly needed a drink.

What he didn't know was that Adele had witnessed the whole incident from her room in the National Hotel. The singer was dumbfounded by the sudden and violent confrontation. Two men lying dead in the street shot down by her husband. The blood-curdling sight appalled her. And he had almost killed the third bushwhacker.

Reasons for the sudden violence were irrelevant to Adele's way of thinking.

Merely the fact that Cal Bonner was once again in the thick of the action was all that counted. She turned away, unable to comprehend the enormity of the occurrence.

This was what she had run away from all those years before. Yet here she was, still holding a candle for the guy. How could she have been so naïve to think that Cal would have changed his ways? And he never would, that was for sure. All his talk of settling down was just that, nothing but hot air to wheedle his way back into her bed.

* * *

Tilly Dumont's contract at the Crystal Chandelier would be finished by the end of the week. She had made up her mind to leave. And alone. A ticket on the first stagecoach leaving Wichita the day after her final performance was the only answer. Standing by the open window, head in hands, the anguish flooded out. Tears of resentment mingled with an intense heartbreak. Her hand strayed to the wedding ring kept on a gold chain around her neck. In a fit of rage, she tore it off and flung it into a corner.

But Adele was not the only one to have been privy to the shoot-out. A certain croupier was already making plans to leave town. Candy Flowers was in a fit of panic following the failure of her lethal plot. The mush inside her head was quickly pushed aside as the instinct for survival took over.

She had no intention of being around when the nickel dropped. It was only due to her ex-beau's refusal to heed Snake Jarman's cowardly attempt to blow the whistle that he was still in the dark as to the real reason for the call-out. But it would not take long for Cal Bonner to figure out her part in the devious plot.

Candy was also wondering how she could have been so stupid. Although her concern was for a very different reason to that of her adversary. Hiring those inept cowboys to do a gunman's job was the height of foolishness. Now she was a hundred bucks down along with any satisfaction she might have fleetingly gained from a different result. Flight was the only course of action open to her.

Cal's addled brain was still recovering from the brutal showdown when a sharp cry cut through the stilted hush that always seemed to follow a spate of intense violence. For a moment the panic-laden holler failed to register. A second, more strident call dug away the sludge. 'Cal, Cal!! Behind you. That guy is after finishing the job!'

From her elevated position, Tilly had been accorded a clear view of the whole street from end to end. Her eyes had instinctively followed the pardoned man as he galloped off only to swing down an intersection three blocks west. Her eyes crinkled in puzzlement. Why had he not left town completely?

Moments later she had the answer. Freedom from certain death had resurrected Bob Jarman's rattled nerves, along with the bravado to avenge his sidekicks. He had not been named the Snake-Eyed one in error. The dry-gulcher lurched back into view. Knees tightly gripped the flanks of his horse to leave him free to shoulder an old Henry repeater. The carbine was clutched in both hands, a frigidly piercing gaze latching onto the stooped object of his opprobrium.

On sighting his quarry, the potential killer levered a shell into the breech and snapped off a couple of shots. But a galloping horse was no place to achieve accuracy in shooting. Three more bullets chewed the ground on either side of the intended victim. Jarman's all-consuming prerequisite had spoiled his aim.

After the first shot, Cal's experience leapt into action. A dive to his left saw the lawman scrambling behind a water trough where he was able to take a bead on the charging rider. His right arm was aching from Wyoming Bill's bullet wound. He hoped the left would not fail him.

The first shot clipped Jarman's arm, throwing his aim even further off course. Yet still he came on, shouting and balling to maintain his courage. A malevolent compulsion had gripped the very essence of his being.

But the advantage had now shifted to the defender. With one Navy empty, Cal flipped the second fully loaded pistol into his good hand — a manoeuvre taught him by Wild Bill and known as the Denver Shift. Three rapid-fire shots blasted off. So fast was the finger action they sounded like a single discharge. Black powder smoke pulsed from the barrel as the deadly trio took Bob Jarman in the chest.

A single hair-raising 'Aaaaaaaaagh!' issued from the constricted throat as the dead man threw up his arms and tumbled from the saddle.

So it was that three dead men now lay sprawled out on the street after all. Cal slowly lumbered to his feet and stood there swaying as he took in the scattered remnants of battle. Kingman looked like a demented house painter had gone crazy with a tin of soldier red. He was standing outside the Prairie Dog.

A side door in the adjacent passage opened and Candy Flowers emerged. She peered around the corner of the building. Here was her chance to finish the job she ought never to have delegated to those bungling greenhorns.

A quick glance around. Nobody else was on the street. All were doubtless cowering in their pits. Candy sneered. Well, the killing was not over yet. The town's yellow streak would work to her advantage. What she had in mind would give the good citizens of Wichita much to think on. Cautiously she stepped out into the open. Her right hand gripped the small Wesson pocket gun. Coarse lines of anger tightened the natural contours of her face into a mask of hatred.

His shoulders hunched, the still

figure standing beside the water trough had not moved a muscle. A bullet in the back held no feeling of guilt for the vengefully scorned croupier. The gun rose, pointing directly at the marshal's spine, no more than ten feet away. But the bullets were never released.

The sharp bite of hot lead took the girl in the neck. Only seconds later another slug bit deep into the side of her face. Candy stood there swaying for a moment as blood poured from the fatal wounds. Then she tumbled into the dirt.

Once again Cal Bonner spun around, his smoking Navy panning the street. Disbelief loomed from hooded eyes as he stared at the still form of his old flame.

In the middle of the street, Tilly Dumont burst into tears. She tossed aside the empty Derringer. Both hands held her face in a manic clasp as the terrible notion of what she had been forced to do struck home. Like a flash of lightning, Cal imbibed the whole situation. He hurried across to comfort his one true love.

For a moment she was transfixed by the horror of the situation before the awful reality struck home. Emitting a scream of anguish she thrust him off.

'Leave me alone!' she blurted out in frenzied angst. 'This is what you have brought me to. A killer, no better than you or those you seek to destroy. I want nothing more to do with you. I'll be leaving Wichita as soon as my contract is finished.' The imploring look from her husband provoked a spirited after-thought. 'And before you ask, I'll be alone. Even though I want nothing more to do with you, Perry Blaine certainly has no place in my life.'

More floods of tears burst forth. An impassable river that found the equally distraught lawman impotent to ease her pain. It was left to the Widow Gillett to lead the distressed figure away.

'You come with me, my dear,' she gently cajoled the weeping girl. 'You can stay at my place for as long as you want.' Her critical remark that followed was for the sole benefit of the isolated lawman. 'I'm sure the marshal has plenty to occupy his time until after you have left town.'

6

Lobo

Cal Bonner was slumped in his office chair. The street had been cleaned up. Folks were going about their business in a subdued manner. That did not prevent nervous looks being cast at the law office by those who walked past. The object of their disquiet was halfway through a new bottle of bourbon. He kept looking at his hands expecting them to be coated in blood.

Bear River Cal was no stranger to gunfighting. Yet each time death left its calling card, a part of him was also left behind. And it didn't get any easier having to live with that fact. Unlike many of those who had tried to end his career, killing and its aftermath haunted his dreams. Yet he had never faltered in pursuing that intuitive passion to rid

96

the western territories of their lawless elements.

But this recent fracas was far worse than any others to which he had been a party for obvious reasons. Cal had sadly misjudged the vengeful retaliation of spurning a girl like Candy Flowers. Now she was dead. And it would have been his bloodied corpse lying in the street had not Adele saved his own life. The one woman he thought was lost forever had come to his aid. How must she be feeling having been forced into making that choice? One life for another. More to the point, had such a catastrophic decision ruined his chances of that reconciliation he thought was on the cards? The whole sorry episode had shaken him to the core. That mission to uphold the principles of decent living was now under close scrutiny.

The fact that his reputation as a tough lawman could be at stake when word spread that Cal Bonner had been at the centre of an ignoble affair of the heart passed over his head. Let folks think what they liked. Cal didn't give a hoot. He was more concerned with the heavy burden of culpability his wife now bore. Was this to be the end of that fresh start before it had even begun?

Another slug of bourbon disappeared down his throat. Head in hands, he knew that retrospection regarding his unsavoury behaviour would achieve nothing. He needed to see Adele and somehow try to salvage the shattered remnants of their marriage before it was too late.

Before leaving the jailhouse, he reloaded his guns and selected a twelve gauge shotgun from the rack, stuffing a handful of cartridges into his pockets. There might well be others out there eager to try their luck at gunning down the well-known town tamer. On the boardwalk he met Doc Bailey who had come to check up on the shoulder wound of Browny Jagus.

'You'll have to give that a miss for now, Doc,' Cal informed the sawbones.

'I have to see Miss Dumont. Try and persuade her to hear me out.'

'You sure have an uphill struggle there, Cal.' The medic's tone was morose, less than encouraging, and laced with disapproval. It was definitely not the kind of censure Cal wanted to hear. 'What in thunderation have you gotten yourself involved in? Sparking a roulette croupier like Candy Flowers while still married to a classy lady like Tilly Dumont.'

'How do you know about that?' the startled badge-man shot back, pulling up short. 'I ain't told nobody else. In any case, my personal affairs are no concern of your'n, Doc.' The irked marshal made to elbow the medic aside. 'Now if'n you don't mind, I'm in a hurry.'

But Doc Bailey was not so easily rebuffed. 'It was when the Widow Gillett asked me to check Tilly out after the shooting. The poor girl was in a right state. I had to give her a sedative to calm her down. She told me all about why she came to Wichita.' The medic's lip curled disdainfully. 'You disappoint me, Cal. I had you down as a straight-up kind of guy. Maybe I was wrong.'

'If'n you must know,' Cal relented, figuring the doctor had a right to know the truth, 'I had no idea that Adele — that's her real name — was coming to Wichita. She left me some years ago when I refused to abandon the law. But when I saw her get off that stage, I knew deep down there was only one woman for me.' His face sagged at the thought of how things had panned out.

'So where did Candy fit into your plans?'

'She was never going to be anything more than a bit of fun to me.' The marshal heaved a deep sigh of regret before adding, 'The poor gal obviously saw it in a different light. And I have to live with that.'

A sagacious look redolent of his advanced years creased the doc's visage. His response held a more appreciative undertone. 'Women take affairs of the heart very seriously as you've found to your cost.'

Cal nodded accepting his naïvety in the situation. 'Guess I should have been more understanding. Somehow she must have learnt about me and Adele and taken it badly. So bad she was prepared to gun me down in the back. Adele saved my life. And for that I owe her an explanation. That's where I'm going now.'

Doc Bailey clapped a benevolent hand on the lawman's shoulder. 'You have my sympathy, Cal. And I wish you luck. You are going to need it.' He sucked in a deep lungful of air before adding. 'When I was down there just now, she was adamant about leaving town.'

Over in his office above the Prairie Dog saloon, Cody Meek was seething. Three rannies had been gunned down in the street after they called Bonner out. Not only that, his best croupier had herself been shot by the singer his partner was supposedly going to marry. More important, that damned tinstar was still walking the streets.

The saloon boss was pacing the floor in agitation when the door burst open to admit his business associate, who was likewise in a state of heightened agitation.

'I just heard about Tilly shooting your croupier,' Blaine lambasted his partner. His arms were waving about like a flag in the wind. 'Do you know anything about it? Why in hell's name should she have done something like that out of the blue? It don't make no sense.'

'According to one of the other girls, Candy was hoping for more than Bonner was prepared to offer,' Meek replied pouring them both a liberal shot of Scotch. 'When those cowpokes failed to take him down, she saw red and tried to complete the job.'

'That don't explain why Tilly butted in.'

'You've been going round with your

head so far in the clouds over that gal, you ain't seen what was obvious to me. And everybody else in town for that matter.' Meek sipped his drink before launching his kick in the teeth. 'Bonner and her have a history that goes way back.'

'What are you getting at, buddy?' Blaine snapped angrily. 'Just spit it out.'

'The two of them are still married.'

The theatre owner was flabbergasted. 'What? That can't be true. You're lying. She would have told me.' He made to grab hold of Meek.

But the wily saloon boss side-stepped. A small pocket pistol, an American Arms .32, appeared in his hand. 'Stay back, Perry. This little beauty is loaded,' he warned his snarling associate. 'Now simmer down and listen up good before we both do something we'll regret.' He waited until Blaine had recovered his composure. 'One of the other croupiers passed me the word. Candy confided her suspicions to Riva Speedwell.' Meek assumed a look of commiseration. 'Looks like

Tilly has been playing you for a sucker, pard. I'm sorry.'

Blaine's anger soon coalesced into a burning urge to even the score. Thin pinpricks of black hate glowed beneath the bushy eyebrows. He snatched up the glass of whisky and tossed it back before he poured out another that went the same way. 'Its about time that skunk learned that he ain't running this town. We are. And I'm gonna make sure that message is delivered in the only way he understands.'

'How do you intend doing that, Perry?' Meek said, pocketing his gun now that the danger to his continued good health had passed. 'The guy has more lives than a cat. And he proved it yet again down on Kingman.'

'Remember when I mentioned that I could have the answer to our problem with Bonner?' Meek frowned but gave a perfunctory nod. 'Well I know just the guy who would like nothing more than to put the critter's lights out permanently.'

* * *

The person to whom Perry Blaine had referred was at that very moment idly playing patience in a Denver saloon. Originally known as *Lobo Solitario* due to his preference for working alone, the nickname had been shortened to Lobo for convenience.

He was the product of a liaison between a Mescalero squaw and a Mexican trader. Pancho Valdez sold guns to the warring Apaches for the purpose of driving the hated white-eyes from their lands. The shifty gun runner disappeared soon after the birth, taking the child with him. The brief coupling had given young Miguel a distinctive swarthy appearance. Later in adulthood it had been accompanied by the traditional drooping moustache favoured by Mexican *bandidos*.

Early in life the half breed had learned the hard way that no faction willingly accepted such a disparate inheritance. Young Miguel had proved to be an adept partner to his father's nefarious activities. But Pancho made a poor parent. A heavy-handed manner found him paying the ultimate price. One too many beatings suffered by him and his younger brother eventually pushed Miguel over the edge. The die was cast. Destiny had spoken. He had made his first killing by the age of fifteen. A life on the run was inevitable.

Accepted neither by red man nor white, Miguel and Chico drifted north unable to settle in one place for long. They tried their hands at farming. But scratching a precarious living on a dirt farm did not sit well with the Valdez brothers. Surely there had to be easier ways of earning a crust. The two boys had robbed stores before graduating to stagecoaches in Arizona.

They had been forced to part company after one failed robbery when Miguel was caught and thrown into jail. The enterprising *bandido* had escaped two days later by climbing up a chimney inside his cell.

He had drifted further north up into

Nevada where the Comstock Lode had turned Virginia City into the territory's mining metropolis. The area offered easy pickings for an enterprising dude. His first chance came when a ruthless land grabber hired him to 'persuade' gold prospectors to abandon their claims. It proved to be a successful undertaking and a new career was born.

Other jobs quickly followed. And they were many and varied. So long as they paid well, the gunman had no qualms regarding their purpose. Inside or outside the law, it made no difference to the ruthless predator who had earned his nickname by a dogged persistence in stalking his prey. In actuality he favoured illicit work which was much more lucrative.

Most jobs involved the removal of business rivals. Others were in the protection racket. Acting as bodyguard to the well-connected was particularly favoured being high-status and espe-cially profitable. Thus was born the infamous name of Lobo.

Business was rather slack at the moment in the Long Tom, which was not to the wolfman's liking. He much preferred to be active and that meant keeping his gun hand well exercised.

Neither of the two Valdez boys had set eyes on each other for over five years, although recently Miguel had received an apologetic letter from Chico that had been resting in a Nevada post office for upwards of six months before he claimed it. Apparently his brother had gravitated into the business of bounty hunting.

And he also had abandoned his Mexican name in favour one more suited to his newfound calling — one that suited his hair colour, unusual for a Mexican, and the creek beside which he was camping at the time . . . *Browny Jagus!*

7

Gun for Hire

As its name indicated, the Long Tom was populated primarily by gold prospectors hoping to sell their hard-earned paydirt, or grab a stake in the latest strike up in the hills west of Denver. Grainy photographs of the lucky few graced the tobacco-stained walls. Most of the miners were only able to scrape a meagre living from their claims. It soon became clear that only the larger enterprises were scooping the big takes. But such is the insatiable lure of the yellow peril that a constant procession of new hopefuls arrived in the town on a daily basis.

The saloon had become Lobo's base since pulling off his last job over the border in the South Dakota county of Shannon. An old friend of the gunslinger's had needed help to get rid of a thorn in his side. A particularly meddlesome Indian agent had been giving Murdo Belvedere grief over tainted meat sold to the Oglala Sioux on the Pine Ridge reservation.

Lobo smiled at the recollection as he poured himself another shot of tequila.

On the day in question he had tailed the agent, one Phineas Witten, who had left the town of Porcupine with the intention of challenging Belvedere at his trading post on the edge of the Badlands. Both men arrived at the post within a few minutes of each other. When Lobo entered the rough-hewn log cabin, Witten was berating his buddy for buying old meat discarded by various butchers in Shannon county, and then selling it on as prime beef to the Indians.

'Howdie there, Lobo, old buddy,' enthused Belvedere when the gunslinger entered the cabin. 'Ain't seen you in a coon's age. How you been doing?'

'Better than you it seems,' replied the wily critter, throwing a disparaging glower towards the only other occupant. 'This fella giving you grief?'

'He claims the meat I'm selling to Crazy Dog and his people is unfit for human consumption. Did you ever hear such a downright lie?' The unscrupulous trader squared his shoulders in vexation at the slur on his reputation. 'I'm telling you straight, Mr Witten, my goods are fit for white folks' dining tables, let alone redskins. Ain't that the goldarned truth, Lobo?'

'I'll vouch for that, Murdo,' the gunman said in support of his associate. 'And to prove it, I'll eat one of those steaks along with this guy to show there's nothing wrong with them. You up for that, Witten? I've known this man a long time and he's straight as a Sunday school teacher. There's no way I'm gonna poison myself by eating bad meat.'

Both men looked to Phineas Witten for his reaction to the challenge. The agent rubbed his stubble-coated jaw uncertain of his ground. He only had the word of Crazy Dog that the meat was inedible. Could the Oglala chief be trying to undermine his authority? If this guy was prepared to eat it, how could he refuse?

'OK, I agree to the proposal,' he finally agreed after due consideration. 'But only if Belvedere allows me to choose my own cut.'

'I have no problem with that,' the trader quickly concurred. 'And to show I ain't holding no grudges, I won't charge either of you. All my goods are legit.'

'Make sure you give us both an extra helping of fried potatoes and green beans,' Lobo added, 'seeing as it's on the house. Reckon you're going to be eating humble pie for dessert, fella. I can vouch for Murdo.'

'I trust that you are right, sir,' replied the somewhat bewildered agent.

The trader went into the kitchen to give the order to his cook. The squaw was a member of the Kiowa tribe who were sworn enemies of the Sioux. Her boss gave a sly wink. She knew exactly what to do. Extra seasoning to hide the taste of the bad stuff.

Fifteen minutes later the food was placed on the table in front of the two diners by Wind that Talks. 'This sure looks good,' Lobo waxed lyrical palming his knife and fork. 'Makes a guy slaver just looking at it. And some tinned corn as well. Much obliged, Wind.' The Indian girl coloured. She was unused to praise.

He was about to dig in with gusto when Witten stayed his hand. 'I seem to recall having the option to choose my own meal.' He leaned across to exchange plates with his fellow diner. 'You have no objections, I take it, Mr Lobo?'

The gunman shrugged. 'None whatsoever, sir,' he replied with a wide grin. 'It was no idle boast that Murdo here is honest as the day is long.'

Both men then got stuck into their

food. Nothing untoward occurred until five minutes after the meal was concluded and the Indian agent was enjoying a cigar. 'Guess I was wrong about you, Belvedere,' he apologized. 'I must have got it all wrong. I'm sorry for doubting you. That skulking rat Crazy Dog is going to be in big trouble for trying to hoodwink me.'

The words had barely left his lips when his face creased in pain. The blood drained from his face. Both hands grabbed at his stomach as he pitched over onto the floor. Groaning and retching he curled up into a ball desperately trying to stop the savage attack on his innards. His face turned green, eyes rolling up into his head.

'Ugggh! Eeeeek!' Croaking groans of agony issued from a gaping mouth.

'Mr Witten doesn't seem too well, Murdo,' the gunman casually enunciated watching the frantic performance on the floor. 'Do you think he might have eaten something that hasn't agreed with him?'

'Could be, Lobo. But I can't for the life of me think what's caused it.' Both men shook their heads in mock commiseration. The ruse had gone exactly as planned.

'Me neither. Surely not tainted meat,' exclaimed the shocked gunslinger.

'Reckon there's only one cure for what's ailing him,' the trader announced.

The two buddies aimed lurid grins down at the writhing form on the floor. Then they roughly hauled the agent to his feet and marched him outside over to a deep ravine. Before he knew what was happening Phineas Witten had taken to the air. A keening howl followed the duped Indian agent down into the angry depths of Bear-in-the-Lodge Creek.

The two men shook hands. 'Looks like there's going to be a vacancy for a new Indian agent in Shannon county,' Belvedere declared, a satisfied smirk cloaking his devious visage.

'And I know the ideal guy for the

job,' Lobo said approvingly nodding towards a bottle of the best Scotch whisky reserved for special occasions. 'Reckon this calls for a drink to celebrate your good fortune.'

Murdo Belvedere had rewarded his sidekick's assistance in the appropriate manner. But that dough was fast disappearing. He flipped another card over just as a little bald-headed dude sporting a green eyeshade pushed open the batwing doors of the saloon. Chickweed Parmalee eyed the bustling throng over his pince-nez spectacles before pushing through the crowd to where Lobo was seated.

'A cable just arrived for you,' the telegraph clerk said, handing over the scrawled message. 'Not more than ten minutes ago. Reckon it sounded urgent.'

Lobo remained silent while he read the brief message. 'You did right, Chickweed,' he responded, flipping a quarter into the air which the clerk deftly snatched. 'I'll be over soon for you to send the reply.'

Again he read the cable teasing out the hidden meaning behind the innuendo. WELL PAID JOB AVAILABLE IN WICHITA, KANSAS, FOR AN ENTERPRISING MAN WITH INITIATIVE. THE JOB INVOLVES REMOVAL OF VERMIN FROM THE TOWN. It was signed Perry Blaine, Waste Disposal Superintendent.

The gunslinger couldn't help laughing out loud. It emerged more as a rasping cackle. A group of nearby prospectors looked round. They quickly moved away. Lobo's reputation was renowned throughout the mining camps of Colorado. Nobody wanted to antagonize the notorious hard case. Lone Wolf was an apt description that fitted the guy like a glove. And that laugh did not sound like the response to a joke. The space that opened around him reeked of anxiety.

'Don't worry, boys,' the gunman exclaimed, allaying their fears. 'This message has put me in a good mood.'

117

A collective sigh of relief rippled through the massed ranks of sweaty miners as the tension evaporated. Men immediately resumed their discussion about the latest silver strike over in Buffalo Gulch. Lobo's mind was taken up with the coded missive. It was clearly from some guy who needed his expertize to get rid of a rival. Again the hired gunman smiled at the ingenuity of the sender.

Most requests for his kind of work came by word of mouth or letter. Sending cables was a risky business. Too many outsiders were able to read the contents. Coded messages were, therefore, essential to prevent unwelcome attention from lawdogs when the particular job in question was below the parapet. Mr Blaine was clearly one of this kind. But his choice of insinuation was more inventive than most.

And it had certainly piqued Lobo's curiosity. Removing a pencil from behind his ear, the gunman scrawled his reply on the back of the cablegram.

JOB SOUNDS RIGHT FOR MY COMPANY TO TACKLE. EXPECT ARRIVAL IN WICHITA WITHIN THE NEXT WEEK. L. WOLFENDEN — PEST CONTROLLER.

★   ★   ★

Lobo made good time across the rolling grassland of eastern Colorado and into Kansas. An endless sea of dull green as far as the eye could see. In stark contrast to the mountainous west it spurred him onward. A week of this and he was more than relieved to reach the burgeoning settlement on the banks of the Arkansas River. Open grassland here was covered by a sea of brown. Milling longhorns that were awaiting sale and delivery to the holding pens on the edge of the town.

The haunting refrain of a locomotive whistle impinged on his thoughts as another line of empty trucks arrived from the east ready to fill up with prime beef on the hoof. Lobo couldn't help but be impressed. This was his first visit to Kansas. He had heard tell of the booming cattle industry. But this was his first experience of how important it had become.

There was clearly a lot of dough to be made in bergs like this. The hired gunman rode into the outskirts of the town wondering about who was going to be facing the sharp end of his six shooter. It had to be somebody of note for Perry Blaine to have summoned him all the way from Denver. His first task would be to seek out the guy and hear what he had to say, and more importantly, how much he was willing to pay.

Fixing his plainsman hat straight, Lobo stuck a cheroot between his teeth. A vesta scratched across the saddle horn flared, revealing a granite-hewn face. Blue smoke dribbled lazily from the corner of the gunman's mouth while he surveyed the bustling thoroughfare.

The first saloon he encountered on

Kingman Street was the Troubadour. Lobo guided the paint over to the hitching rail and tied up alongside a half-dozen range mustangs. The cowboys must be in town. Although they could have been attending a temperance convention, judging by the lack of noise. The gunman's face wrinkled up into a bewildered frown.

He had been expecting a far more raucous welcome. From what he had heard about these jaspers after a trail drive, all hell broke loose when they hit town. The place was more akin to a cemetery. No gunfire, or horses galloping up and down the street. That was in sharp contrast to the bustling huddle of buildings on the opposite bank of the Arkansas. He could hear the racket even from this side of the river. Something about Wichita didn't feel right at all.

The sooner he ran Blaine to ground the better. And who better to ask as to his whereabouts than a bartender. And so it proved. Within ten minutes of arriving in town, Lobo was ushered into the inner sanctum of Perry Blaine at the rear of the Crystal Chandelier. Another guy was with him. Both potential employers studied the newcomer closely before speaking.

Cody Meek attempted to overawe the gunman with a lofty disdain that tried unsuccessfully to express his pre-eminence in the forthcoming events. Lobo held the gambler's watery gaze with a jaundiced disregard. It was Meek who was forced to look away. Blaine's attitude was much more relaxed. He needed this guy and wanted to keep him on side.

It was he who stepped forward to greet their intended associate.

'You made good time, Lobo,' he said holding out a welcoming hand which Lobo ignored. Nothing had been agreed as yet. And until the right price was forthcoming, the gunman had no intention of succumbing to any flummery exuding from these smooth talking jaspers. The fixed smile pasted across the impresario's oily face slipped. Momentarily nonplussed by the snub, it quickly returned as the loose hand disappeared into a pocket. 'You must be plum tuckered out after such a long ride. I've fixed you up with a room at the National Hotel. I trust that will be satisfactory?'

Lobo continued to ignore the unctuous remarks. Instead, he tossed aside his half-smoked cheroot and selected a fine Havana from the humidor on Blaine's desk. After getting it going to his liking, the gunman helped himself to a shot of finest Scotch whisky before deigning to address his two potential employers. 'I see you guys only keep the good stuff. You must be making a healthy living in this dump. So what kind of vermin is it that you want exterminating?'

A shrewd operator, Blaine quickly surmised which way the conversation was heading. He likewise lit up a cigar offering the gun toter a studied appraisal. After all, it was they who were employing him and not the other way around. He wandered over to a drinks cabinet and poured himself a measure of French brandy. Sipping it with an expert deliberation he then laid out the proposition.

'This town as you might have noticed already is rather quiet at the moment. Much too quiet as far as my colleague and I are concerned. Sure, we're doing OK. But not nearly as well as we should be.'

Cody Meek gave the remark a spirited nod of accord. 'There's plenty of money to be made from all the trail herds coming up from Texas . . . '

' . . . but the cowboys don't like the fact that Wichita has been placed under a no-gun ruling by the town marshal,' added Blaine.

'And on top of that,' Meek cut in again, 'all places of entertainment have to close up by midnight, even at weekends. Once they come up against all these damn blasted rules they start drifting over the river to Delano where 'anything still goes.'

'So I noticed,' the newcomer remarked nonchalantly.

'Wichita used to be like that,' Blaine continued, 'and we want those days back which means getting rid of the starpacker.'

Lobo couldn't contain a bout of ribald laughter.

'What's so danged funny?' Meek hollered out. 'This ain't no joke, mister.'

'You guys are like a stage double act. You crease me up.' He slapped his left thigh gleefully.

But Perry Blaine was not fazed. He still had an ace up his sleeve and played it with panache. 'You won't be so offhand when I tell you the name of this tinstar. I have a distinct feeling you've come across him before.' Blaine deliberately paused holding the other man's gaze, knowing that Lobo was hanging fire for the revelation. The showman was an expert when it came to working an audience.

The cutting retort had the desired effect. Lobo's cynical joviality evaporated like money from a cowboy's pocket.

'So are you gonna spill or not?' the gunman rasped out, trying to keep the curiosity from his retort.

'Ever heard of a guy called . . . Bear River Cal Bonner?'

The wide-eyed stare told the two men all they needed to know. 'And we're prepared to offer you 2,000 bucks to remove him from the picture.'

Lobo turned around to hide the shock cloaking his swarthy features. He twirled the long moustache while walking across the room to pour himself another drink. Such a disclosure needed a liberal shot before any response could be given. Extracting a handkerchief from his back pocket he casually buffed the conchos lining his black leather vest. It was a reflex action that gave him time to consider this startling revelation.

'Two grand?' the gunman eventually

coughed out. 'Is that all? Don't seem much to me for the extra trade I'm going to be bringing in by removing this jasper.'

'Make it three then,' Meek interrupted, panic clawing at his throat. 'But that's as far as we're going.'

Lobo hawked out a mirthless guffaw. 'You guys sure are eager to have your town back. Seems to me the kind of help I can offer deserves a much higher reward. Especially when you're calling for the removal of Cal Bonner.'

Blaine stiffened. He had a brooding suspicion where this was heading. 'You can't hold us to ransom. There are other guys out there who would do this for half what we're offering.'

'So where are they?' The scornful demand received no answer, merely a pair of frustrated grimaces. 'I thought not. Cal Bonner is no greenhorn as I'm sure you've already discovered. You could send for another hired gun, but that could take time. And he'd just as likely pick up the same drift as me.'

'Get to the point, Lobo,' Meek rapped out. 'What are you really after?'

'Nothing too much. Just an equal share in the business you guys have going here. Once Bonner is out of the way, I aim to stick around. Reckon I'm gonna like it around here. Especially when you appoint me marshal in his place.'

'That's blackmail,' rasped Meek. 'You can't do that.'

'I just did, and I ain't changing my mind. Now shake on it or I walk.'

'You don't want much, do you?' Blaine exclaimed half-heartedly knowing this guy had them over a barrel.

Lobo shrugged. 'It's just business far as I'm concerned. And we can all make a heap of dough into the bargain. So is it a deal?'

Meek looked somewhat downcast at his partner. They had been herded up a box canyon with only one way out. 'Guess so. But we want the job done quickly. This town has been quiet for too long already.'

The deal was clinched by a hand-shake. 'I'll get over to the hotel and settle in before figuring out my plan of action. See you later . . . pards.'

8

Coal Bank Trickery

In the bar adjacent to the National Hotel later that day, Lobo was to discover something that momentarily left him staggered. Uncharacteristic of the ruthless gunman, he was totally bereft of any reply.

Argo Creede, the barman, was regaling him with the recent attempts by various factions to remove Cal Bonner from the picture. Like all bartenders Argo loved the sound of his own voice. The incident involving Wyoming Bill and his accomplices was explained in all its lurid detail. But it was his final comment that so stunned the hired gunslinger.

'Before those three mossyhorns came to grief outside on the street, some hotshot tried to ambush the marshal while he was in the barber's shop.' The barman chuckled to himself. 'That guy didn't stand a chance against a sharp cookie like Cal Bonner. The marshal took him down with his eyes closed — cool as you please just sitting in the barber's chair. And he did it with a Derringer. Clipper Jim told me all about it.'

'This fella seems like one real tough *hombre*,' declared Lobo sipping his beer. He struggled not to let his disdain show.

'You can say that again,' the appreciative beer-tapper advocated with relish. 'He's managed to make this town fit for decent folks to live in.'

'And single-handedly as well,' added a dark-suited guy further down the bar. 'Hiring Bear River Cal was the best appointment the town council ever made. Although there are some in Wichita who would prefer he was a permanent resident in the cemetery.'

'You talking about those saloon

johnnys across the street, Doc?' said Creede.

'I sure am. And there are more like them as well,' the medic advocated, taking a gentle sip of sherry.

'Well, their kind ain't welcome in the National,' blustered Creede, stamping his foot to emphasize his support for the current regime.

Lobo maintained a neutral demeanour. They were clearly referring to the jaspers with whom he had hooked up. It seemed that in the National Hotel bar at least Bonner still had enough support to keep a lid on things.

'That bushwhacker sure learned the hard way that going up against the marshal is bad for your health.'

'And you should know about that, eh Doc? Is the bushwhacking skunk fit enough to stand trial yet?' enquired Creede while enthusiastically polishing a glass. 'I heard he'd taken a slug in the shoulder.'

'The circuit judge ain't due for

another month,' replied Doc Bailey. 'But he'll be well enough to serve a good long term in the state pen at Leavenworth by then.'

'It might make him see the error of his ways,' commented the barman.

The medic shook his head. 'Guys like that never learn. Sure as that hair on your head came out of a box, Argo, they always end up face down in the mud just like those foolish cowpokes.'

Creede's hand automatically lifted to his head. A hurt look graced his rubicund features. 'Hey! No need to tell the whole world, Doc,' protested the self-conscious barkeep. 'This peruke was hand made in St Louis. Cost me all of fifty bucks.'

'They saw you coming,' said Lobo, joining in the hilarity.

'A pity Browny Jagus didn't have more sense as well,' remarked Doc Bailey finishing his drink. 'Anyway, I'll be off on my rounds now, Argo. No rest for the pure in heart.' And with that unconscious parting shot across the bows, Doc Bailey departed leaving Lobo ashen-faced. The gunman clutched at the bar rail to stop himself falling over. Such was the shock of learning that his own brother had been the topic of conversation.

'Something wrong, mister?' the concerned barman enquired. 'You look like you've lost a gold watch and found a dime.'

The hired gunman quickly fought off the dizziness threatening to engulf him. 'Just a bit tired is all. Guess I need some sleep after my hard ride to get here.'

The answer appeared to satisfy Argo Creede. He splashed a measure of brandy into a glass. 'Drink this down. It'll soon clear your head. And it's on the house seeing as you're a guest in the hotel.'

'Much obliged.' Lobo nodded his thanks slinging the shot down in one gulp. 'Boy, I sure needed that.'

But not for the reason you're thinking, *compadre*, he thought. The notion that his brother had attempted and failed miserably to do the job he himself was now contemplating was difficult to absorb. But getting shot up and facing imprisonment — it was a lot to take in. His cheeks flushed as the hard liquor took a hold. But the snort had done its work. Gone was the glassy-eyed look. Instead it was replaced by an ice-cold glint that spoke of dire retribution heading in the direction of Bear River Cal Bonner.

Now Lobo had two reasons for ridding the world of that fluke-ridden chancer. And he was going to enjoy every goldarned second watching his life blood drain away. This was no longer just another paid job of work.

It had become personal. Shooting down both of the Valdez brothers was the worst mistake that skunk had ever made.

'Reckon I'll hit the sack,' the drinker declared, levering himself off the bar.

Hearing the disquieting revelation concerning his brother had shaken

Miguel Valdez to the core. He acknowledged Creed's 'Good night' with a languid wave of the hand and wandered upstairs to his room. Time was needed to reflect on how best to tackle this slippery town tamer.

Throwing off his jacket and hanging the gunbelt on the end of the brass bed head, he lay down. Eyes closed, his mind drifted back some four years. Back to the Animas Valley and the mining boom town of Silverton, Colorado. That was where his fateful clash with Cal Bonner had occurred.

★　★　★

Lobo had drifted east out of Nevada into the mountain fastness of the San Juans seeking a change of scenery. As with most boom towns, the glory days of Virginia City were fading. He was hoping that some of the wealth being dug out of the ground in the new Colorado strikes would find itself into his pockets.

But not as a tenderfoot miner with all the hard grafting that entailed. No sirree! The Comstock had taught him much in the way of skimming off the cream without much effort. And a swift gun hand was the key. Soon after arriving in Silverton, solid written testimonials from previous employers had secured him the job of bodyguard to the owner of the Leopard Skin saloon.

It was in his second week that Lobo overheard a conversation between two miners discussing a recent large gold discovery at the Pandora Mine up in the mountains.

'Old Tom Hickey has sure struck it rich up there,' one grizzled veteran advocated.

'How's he moving the stuff out?' enquired his partner, whose equally wizened face was like hammered bronze.

'He's hired a guard to drive the load down to the smelter in Durango,' came back the sceptical reply.

'Only one guard? He's taking a big chance,' was the jaundiced verdict. 'My bet is some jasper will snatch the lot afore the month is out.'

His buddy nodded in agreement. 'I'll drink to that, pal. And I'll bet you the prize nugget we found in the rocker box last week that the heist will be pulled off at Coal Bank Pass.'

'No chance, pal,' his pard averred firmly. 'I was just about to say that myself.'

That was all Lobo needed to know. Dollar signs flashed before his eyes. Greed and what he judged were easy pickings made up his mind that those two old timers would soon be regaling all and sundry about their dire prediction. No doubt the story would earn them free drinks for a week.

This would be the bodyguard's first foray into outright robbery since he and his brother had parted company. But this caper appeared to be a giveaway — one guard for all that gold? It was almost too good to be true.

And it was just that. What the gunman and the two old timers had failed to realize was that Tom Hickey was no greenhorn miner. He was well aware that there would be lawless factions keen to relieve him of such a lucrative cargo.

Cal Bonner was on his way to Cripple Creek where a vigilance committee needed a more permanent law enforcement officer. He had stopped off at Pandora and got talking to Hickey in the local diner. Bonner's reputation was such that he was hired on the spot for a sizeable fee to transport the load down to the smelter at Durango. It would only take up a brief spell of the lawman's time so he had readily agreed.

Before he set out on the arduous trek down the valley, Hickey offered him a poignant piece of wisdom. 'Take particular care going over Coal Bank Pass. That's where most of the previous trouble has occurred.'

'I'll remember that. Much obliged, Tom,' the starpacker replied, slapping the leathers. 'I'll see you in ten days, all being well. And with a heap of dough.'

'Get back safely and there'll be a bonus in your pay packet.'

'I'll look forward to that.'

On the third day out, the wagon was trundling through the narrow rift which was the highest point of the south-bound trail after leaving Silverton. Cal slowed the wagon down. His muscles tensed knowing this was the danger spot advocated by Tom Hickey. His rifle was resting against his right leg ready for instant use should the need arise. At the same time, a hawkish gaze flicked across the bleak mountain pass. The ravages of time had scored a deep rift through the soaring turrets of rock. On either side massed ranks of aspen and pine clung to the steep slopes offering effective cover for a potential ambusher.

Cal reckoned that a shot from cover would need to be within a hundred yards of its target to ensure a positive hit. A brisk estimate pointed to a cluster of rocks at the head of the pass just before the trail meandered down towards the Hermosa trading post a day's ride beyond. Over to his left, the afternoon sun glinted off the snow-capped Hesperus Summit towering majestically above the remote setting.

But it was a sudden flash of light that caught the haulier's attention. It had come from the rocks he had previously eyeballed as a potential hazard. The short-lived flare could have been anything — glass, a discarded tin can. But suspicion made the lawman focus his gaze. Moments later it happened again at the exact same spot — a reflection made by the sun on what had to be the barrel of a rifle. A trio of jays lifted skyward, squawking at some disturbance in the vicinity. Here was proof in Cal's mind that danger lurked therein.

His face split in a tight smile. 'You were right, old man,' he muttered under his breath. So how to deal with this skulking sidewinder? Another fifty yards and he would be within effective rifle range. He continued onward for as long as he dared before reining the wagon to a halt. The Henry was jammed into his shoulder and a couple of shots despatched in the general direction of the bushwhacker's hideout.

Then he jumped down to shelter behind the wagon. And he was just in the nick of time. Pieces of wood flew every which way, chewed off the wagon by the hidden gunman's retaliation. Now it was a question of playing one of the oldest tricks in the book. But would the critter fall for it?

Removing his hat, Cal stuck it on his rifle and poked the high crown above the wagon rim. It immediately attracted a half-dozen well placed shots that cut the headgear to pieces. A cry of pain rang out, echoing off the rock walls of the pass. Nothing happened for ten minutes. Then the steady pad of approaching feet told Cal that his adversary had taken the bait.

He lay face down on the ground behind the wagon, but with his gun hand hidden and clutching one of his pistols. Seconds felt like hours as the possum feigned death. The boots halted right next to the supposedly dead body.

'Never figured that robbing a gold shipment would be so simple,' the hoodwinked killer breezed, chuckling to himself. 'Easy as taking candy from a baby.' A boot idly reached out to toe the body over onto its back. And that was when Lobo got the shock of his life.

'A sight easier to fool a yellow dog like you, mister,' the cadaver voiced, lifting the pistol. 'They say that the old tricks are the best, but I never thought anybody was stupid enough to fall for it. Seems like there's still one dim-witted asshole around.' The hearty grin dissolved being replaced by a grim resolve. 'Now step back and drop your piece. You're under arrest.'

The gunman reeled back. But he quickly recovered his wits. 'Nobody's taking me in,' he blurted out, lifting the Remington.

Cal's gun spat flame. It was an

accurate shot smashing the pistol in the killer's hand and removing his little finger. Lobo cried out, grabbing at the injured hand. Terror gripped a watching family of rabbits, which scooted back inside their burrow.

The intended victim of the ambush jumped to his feet and laid his revolver across the exposed head of his assailant. With Lobo now out for the count, Cal wrapped the jigger's own bandanna around the bloody stump before trussing him up tighter than a showgirl's corset. The inert hulk was then heaved into the back of the wagon. The stink of burnt powder hung in the air as a heavy silence once again descended over the remote mountain pass.

The winner of the brief showdown sat on a nearby rock and sucked hard on a roll-up to calm his jangling nerves. A belt of whisky from a hip flask also helped to bring his racing heartbeat back to normal. Cal had faced down many guys who had harboured evil intent. But this was the first time he had been attacked from an ambush. Coming out on top was good for morale but hard on the old ticker.

Once he had recovered his composure, Cal climbed back onto the wagon. He slapped the leathers, urging the team of four back into motion. The jolting elicited a groan from the inept bandit who had regained consciousness only to find himself a helpless dupe. Hate-filled eyes peered back at his captor.

'Think on it this way, buster,' Cal intoned cheerily. 'At least you managed to get your wish. Wallowing in a heap of gold. Pity you won't get to spend any of it.' A belt of hollow laughter bounced off the rock walls encompassing the Coal Bank.

9

Bite of the Wolf

Cal was trying to catch up on some paperwork in the office when a knock disturbed the necessary but laborious endeavour. Keeping track of the numerous duties with which a law officer was tasked these days was becoming decidedly irksome. He hadn't signed up to be a pen-pusher. Trial lawyers especially were assiduous in their demands for written evidence.

Browny Jagus was a case in point. His trial was coming up soon. It would have been a sight easier if'n he had just aimed for a killing shot. Far less paperwork and no repercussions. Those prophetic words were to haunt him in the very near future.

Wyoming Bill and his two buddies had been buried in unconsecrated ground the same day of the shooting with only death certificates to sign. An open and shut case witnessed by numerous onlookers. Candy Flowers, however, was a different matter. Cal still had to interview Adele for her side of the incident, which didn't bode well for his involvement in the affair. Mayor Wishart was pressing him to obtain a written testimony as she was threatening to leave town.

He had been deliberately putting it off. Not least because Adele refused to see him. Why did life have to be so complicated? Cleaning up rough mining camps had posed far fewer problems.

'Come in,' the marshal called out, thankful for the rest that his overtaxed brain needed. He threw down the quill pen mouthing an impulsive curse as an ink blot spattered across the accounts ledger. 'Darn it!'

'You don't seem in good spirits, Marshal,' remarked the visitor. Nightjar the stable hand was nervously fingering his hat. 'That's kind of a pity as I ain't the bringer of good news.'

Cal eyed the hovering ostler askance. 'Best spill it then, Nightjar,' he sighed. 'Life don't seem to be getting any easier these days.'

'A mean looking dude just grabbed me outside the National,' the little guy burbled, deeming it wise not to ask for a snort on this occasion. 'He had the look of that Browny Jagus you're holding for trial.' Nightjar swallowed before continuing. This was the time when he could have murdered a shot of the hard stuff. 'Said he'd be waiting for you in the Prairie Dog. The guy didn't give me a name. But he held up his right hand and said you'd know.'

Again Cal's furrowed brow registered incomprehension. 'Quit playing games, fella, and just tell me,' came the snappy riposte.

Another gulp. Nightjar's Adam's apple wobbled. 'His little finger is missing.'

The lawman gripped the chair rests;

his bottom lip fell as the incident at Coal Bank Pass flashed across his mind's eye. A couple of years had passed but the ambush by the gunslinger known as Lobo was still clear as daylight. The varmint must have done his time or escaped and come looking to get even.

Then another thought occurred to the canny lawman. Could he possibly have been hired by Meek and his cronies? They had left him in no doubt that he was the one obstacle thwarting their devious plan to take over Wichita. A narrowed gaze fastened onto the line of wanted dodgers. Lobo was not among them. The guy had somehow managed to keep one step ahead of any illicit conflict with the law.

Nightjar picked up on the starman's disquiet. 'You know this guy, Marshal?'

'We've had dealings,' was all he was prepared to divulge. 'Best you keep out of it,' he added standing up and reaching for his gun belt. Next he selected a sawn-off scatter gun slotting two cartridges into the twin barrels of the deadly weapon. There was nothing like being prepared when facing a gunslinger of Lobo's reputation.

Nightjar watched as the hard-boiled lawdog stepped out onto the veranda and began his walk of destiny. It was Saturday. The one day in the week when the sound of revelry ought to be pulsating from every saloon. Yet a sinister quiet had engulfed the town. And it was not merely on account of the strict regulations he had imposed.

News regarding a showdown of this magnitude must have preceded the event itself. It was like a magnet drawing in those of a macabre disposition, ghoulish death seekers who relished the sight of blood being spilled, just so long as it belonged to someone else. Wichita was still not short of such denizens.

Curious eyes followed the marshal as he slowly made his way along the street towards the Prairie Dog on the far side. He crossed over, sensing the presence of his silent audience. It felt like he was entering the Coliseum of ancient Rome, a gladiator fighting to the death for the enjoyment of the crowd.

Sure, he could walk away. The thought of his wife made his step falter. She had threatened to leave on account of his job, and all the baggage it entailed. But his well-deserved standing as a fearless town tamer would then be forfeited. The name of Bear River Cal Bonner would be dragged through the mud, scoffed at in a myriad of saloons from Sadalia down to the Red River. If he was going to surrender his job, then it would be on his terms. Not those of some arrogant hired gunslinger.

His back stiffened with resolve as he paused outside the saloon. Tension you could cut with a knife hung in the air. He sucked in a deep breath. Before he could open the door a hand was laid on his shoulder.

'Nightjar told me about this gunslinger calling you out. You don't have to do this, Cal.' It was Doc Bailey. 'The town would understand.'

The medic's entreaty received a sardonic twist of the lip. 'Would it, Doc? You sure about that? 'Cos I ain't. Turn away now and I'm finished. That's the way it goes in this game. You're only as good as your last face-off.'

He didn't wait for a reaction. Pushing the door open he stepped through into what felt like the jaws of death. The room was full of muttering drinkers. All now turned, looking towards the newcomer standing by the door. The babble faded to a morbid silence. Everyone was fully aware of the imminent confrontation.

Cal returned their gloomy if expectant regard. It was clear that other drinkers whose usual haunts were elsewhere had come to the Prairie Dog in anticipation of a shoot-out. Would their morbid curiosity be assuaged? The next few minutes would decide the issue, one way or another.

Then, just like in the Bible when the waters of the Red Sea parted, the milling throng shifted leaving an empty strip of bare wood down the centre of the room.

And there leaning casually on the empty bar at the far end was the wolf man — *Solitario Lobo*. His teeth were drawn back in a manic rictus. 'Glad you could make it, Marshal,' he spat out. 'These guys are just itching to see how a wolf can pull a bear's teeth.' A manic chuckle echoed around the room. Nobody else joined in. The audience pushed back, eager to keep well out the line of fire that they knew was sure to come.

'Carrying guns within the town limits is banned, Lobo,' the lawman declared, resolutely keeping any quiver out of his utterance. 'Hand them over and we'll say no more about it.'

'I kinda feel a mite naked without them,' the hired gunman heedlessly replied, taking a sip of his whisky. 'Guess you'll have to come and take them. That is if'n you're able. Other tinstars have tried. Wanna guess where they ended up?'

'Same place you're headed if'n you don't surrender them hoglegs,' Cal shot back. 'The graveyard's full of big shots like you.'

'I'm different. You see, Mr Town Tamer, I have an axe to grind.' Lobo held up his four-digit hand while lighting a cigar. The crowd gasped causing the atmosphere in the saloon to palpably ratchet up a notch. 'As well as this, you're holding my brother in that jail-house. So it's not only for the money this time.'

Lobo set down his glass and levered himself off the bar. In the flick of a rattler's tongue, his right hand moved. Twice, flame and hot lead spat from the barrel of his Manhattan '36. The ear-splitting discharge blended into a single roar, such was the speed of the slick manoeuvre. Lobo had been practising a while for this very moment. He knew that Cal Bonner was no slouch with a pistol so had no intention of offering him the chance to prove it.

That was for suckers.

Black powder smoke mingled with that of tobacco and tallow oil. A collective intake of breath went up from the watching crowd, all eager to witness the result of the showdown. Lobo already knew the outcome. He stumped down the middle of the room and stood over the fallen body of his adversary. A caustic eye checked out the accuracy of his discharge. Satisfaction in the form of a grim smile washed over the brutish features as he peered down at the still form on the floor.

Both slugs had lodged in the victim's chest.

Just to ensure there had been no mistake in his aim, Lobo stamped down hard on Cal Bonner's gun hand. 'Only a fool gives his opponent an even break,' he snarled out. 'Too bad you never learned that lesson, Marshal.' The crack of bone sent shivers of dread through those watching. Lobo merely smiled. It was more akin to a wolf's snarl. The recipient of the malicious piece of brutality never moved a muscle.

'That's just in case you figured on playing possum.' Following this callous reasoning behind the vicious act, the killer's gun rose to deliver the fatal denouement.

Before he had chance to pull the trigger, Doc Bailey hustled though the door and bent down to examine the still form. 'Stay back and let me examine him,' he ordered, placing his own body between the killer and his victim. The medic's surprising arrival and brusque command momentarily threw the gun-slinger. He moved aside allowing the sawbones to have his way.

'No need for any more of that,' Bailey rasped out moments later following a brisk examination of the victim. Slowly he stood up. The look he gave the hunched killer was chock full of acrimony. 'This man won't be causing you any more problems. So you can put that gun away.'

Bailey quickly glanced around, his

probing gaze searching for a friendly face. Only blank looks stared back at him. The kind of men who fraternized a berg like the Prairie Dog had no love for a lawman that banned the carrying of guns and curtailed their merriment. Then his eyes lit upon a man standing open-mouthed by the door.

'Help me get the marshal's body outside,' he said to the stunned ostler. Nightjar just stood there, transfixed by the sight of the marshal's bleeding corpse. 'Hurry up, man!' the doctor pressed. 'Is your wagon nearby?'

The blunt demand brought the stableman back to life. 'Over th-there,' he stuttered out. 'I was only talking to the poor guy not ten minutes since. I warned him about this fella asking after him . . . '

'Just help me get him into the wagon,' the sawbones butted in. 'And quickly, I need to get him over to the undertaker.'

Before any ghoulish onlookers in the saloon could move to examine the body more closely, the two men hurriedly carried it outside. Bailey jumped up beside the ostler on the bench seat and urged him off up the street. 'Once we're out of sight, head for my surgery,' he ordered the driver.

Nightjar gave the order a quizzical frown. Why not the undertaker's? That was the place for a corpse. But he held his peace. Doc Bailey knew what he was doing. Curiosity, however, won him over once the marshal had been laid down on a bed in the surgical ward. 'What gives, Doc?' he asked, scratching his head. 'Why did you bring him here?'

Even though he was safely ensconced within his own domain, Doc Bailey automatically lowered his voice. 'Can I trust you, Nightjar?' he asked pointedly.

'Of course you can, Doc,' the ostler replied. 'I've always had a high regard for the marshal. He made this town fit for decent folks to live in. I shudder to think what'll happen now he's dead.'

Bailey's voice sank even lower such that Nightjar strained to listen in.

'That's the whole point of this charade. He ain't dead at all. Not yet anyway. Those bullets have lodged in his ribs. Although another half inch and he would have been a goner. So you see, I couldn't allow that darned gunslinger to finish the job.'

Nightjar's mouth dropped open in amazement. He stared hard at the blood-stained form splayed out on the bed. 'He sure looks dead,' the sceptical guy declared shaking his head. 'His chest ain't moving. He has to be dead.'

The medic waved a languid hand. 'That's due to shock. His heart has slowed down so that it looks like he's dead. And he will be for certain if'n I don't get to work on him soon.'

Nightjar could only stare back in wonder. He was just a simple guy trying to earn a living. This was beyond his understanding.

The doctor hurried on with his brief explanation. 'Luckily nobody else in the Prairie Dog had the balls to challenge my judgment. Only through luck and you being in the right place at the right time was I able to spirit him away from that plague of locusts.' The medic grabbed the old dude firmly by the arm. 'You won't say anything, will you? This has to remain our secret.'

Even though the stableman was no churchgoer, he crossed himself. 'As God is my witness, you have my word on it, Doc.' He passed a hand over tightly compressed lips. 'Silence is golden.'

The medic emitted a deep sigh of relief. 'But he can't stay here. It's fortunate that today is my nurse's day off. But she'll be in tomorrow. And I don't want to answer any awkward questions. The fewer people that know about this the better. He's badly hurt and his mashed hand needs attention as well. I'm just praying that he ain't too far gone. It's gonna be touch and go. But if'n he does pull through, he'll need somewhere to rest up during his recovery. Any ideas?'

Nightjar considered the request carefully before voicing his opinion.

'There is a place I know of that ain't visited anymore.'

'Where is it?' The medic was all ears now.

'An old buffalo hunter called Skinny Jim Flint built a cabin in Dead Man's Draw north of town. That was when the plains around here were swarming with buffalo. A couple of years back he moved further west along with them migrating woollie-backs. So the place is empty now. We could hide him there.' The ostler was becoming quite enthused by the project. 'I could easily bring in supplies and keep a regular check on his progress once you've seen to the medical side of things.'

'A rather unfortunate choice of name perhaps,' remarked the morose doctor.

'Gee. I never thought about that, Doc,' Nightjar apologized. 'You reckon I should look for someplace else?'

Bailey shook his head. 'No time for

that now. We can only trust in the Good Lord that my skill is sufficient to make it a false omen in the marshal's case. So I suggest you get out there fast and make sure it's fit for the patient to recuperate until he's ready to show his hand. And don't worry about the cost. I'll pay for everything you need and get the money back off the council later.' Already, the doctor had shed his coat and rolled up his sleeves. There was much to be done if he was to save Cal Bonner's life. 'And make sure nobody suspects what you're up to.'

'I'll get out there right away,' opined Nightjar. But the sawbones merely responded with a wave of the hand. His whole attention was now focussed on making sure that the badly injured lawman did not peg out.

Already he had lost a lot of blood, his breathing was shallow and laboured. For the next couple of hours the doctor conjured up all his experience and knowledge of gunshot wounds and bone-setting to tend the injured man.

By the end, he was totally exhausted. 'I'm too darned long in the tooth for this kind of work,' he muttered to himself while cleaning up. A look of resignation creased the world-weary face. 'You're out of my hands now, fella.' His face lifted towards the ceiling. 'Only you, Lord, can decide whether I've done enough.'

A liberal shot of brandy coursed through the medic's frail body. 'Reckon I've earned this whatever happens.' It certainly helped to revive his wilting stamina. There still remained the onerous task of transporting the fragile patient to Dead Man's Draw. A buggy was waiting out back. Already, the celebrations could be heard further along Kingman.

The sawbones scowled. Those critters would be so taken up with their newfound freedom they would forget all about Cal Bonner. This was the best time to head out of town on a back trail. It was lucky that Nightjar had just returned having cleaned up the cabin ready for a hopefully short-lived occupation. Without a second pair of hands, the little doctor would have found it impossible to move the burly lawman on his ownsome.

10

Wide Open

'Drinks are on the house, boys,' declared a delighted Cody Meek, slapping Lobo on the back. 'And it's all because of my new partner here.' A raucous belt of loud cheering greeted this most welcome announcement. 'And don't forget to tell all of your buddies who ain't here that Wichita is once again open for business.'

Eager drinkers surged across to the bar forcing Meek to go behind himself to help the bartenders cope with demand. But he harboured no reluctance. This was a moment to be celebrated.

Lobo helped himself to a bottle of best Scotch. He was more than willing to answer a myriad of queries regarding his prowess in gunplay, even demonstrating a few tricks that had his audience enthralled and gasping with delight. Once the initial sense of euphoria had settled down, he left his new partners busily stocking up support for their takeover bid and made his way across to the jailhouse. The door was wide open. And with nobody in attendance, he walked straight in and over to the cellblock.

'What's all that shooting, Bonner? I thought you had this town locked down tighter than a bank vault.' The sight of his brother in the doorway stunned the prisoner into silence. He was totally lost for words. 'Miguel! It cannot be! Where's Bonner?' he spluttered out. 'Has the skunk caught up with you as well?'

He looked behind his brother fully expecting to see the marshal prodding him into the cell block. Lobo's swarthy face split in a wide grin as he held up a large ring containing the bunch of keys. 'Which one fits your lock? And no, it is no ghost you are seeing. I, Miguel Valdez am now marshal of Wichita. And you, *mi hermano*, are going to be my deputy.'

Chico slumped down on the dirty bunk bed. His head was spinning. 'I think you had better tell me what's happened to deliver such a miracle,' he spluttered, still barely able to credit that he was free.

The selected key grated in the lock allowing the prisoner to leave the cell. They sat down in the main office while Lobo brought his brother up to date with recent events. He then moved across to the scarred desk and searched the drawers.

'I'll get you a room at the hotel.' His nose wrinkled. 'And some fresh duds to go with your new-found status. You smell too much like a dung heap. But first . . . ' The search continued until hisfingers lit upon a shiny metal star with the depiction 'Deputy' engraved thereon. 'Pin that on your vest and raise your right hand. Now say after me.' Chico did as ordered. 'I, Chico Valdez, better known as Browny Jagus, do hereby agree to support my brother Miguel, better known as Lobo, in the pursuit of wealth and all its trappings here in the town of Wichita.'

'Chico Valdez will be greatly honoured to assist his fine brother in such an *excelente* venture,' Jagus espoused after repeating the avowal. 'So Bonner is dead. And we are now in charge of law and order. I like it.' They celebrated with a couple of shots from the bottle left by the alleged dead man. 'He sure ain't gonna miss it. Here's to you, ex-Marshal Bonner, deceased and now stoking the Devil's furnace.'

Glasses were raised followed by hearty guffaws in celebration of this most welcome of outcomes.

'One minute I'm awaiting trial for attempted murder, the next helping to run this town. Life cannot get much better.' Jagus could still barely accept the sudden change in his fortunes. Lady Luck was certainly sitting on his shoulder this day.

After finishing the bottle of bourbon, the self-appointed law officers headed off down the street to the National Hotel. Along the entire length of Kingman, men were whooping and a-hollering. Guns were being fired off into the air. The news that Wichita was once again open for business had spread like wildfire. Even the local mutts got caught up in the jubilation, barking and chasing one another.

Perry Blaine had just emerged from the Prairie Dog. He spotted the two brothers and called across. 'Mind if'n I have a few words with you fellas?' The two men waited for him to cross the street. 'Reckon you must be mighty pleased that your brother decided to take us up on the offer of a partnership, Browny,' he said in feigned innocence, not batting an eyelid. Lobo smirked but made no comment. The impresario held out a hand, which Jagus accepted. 'I'm Perry Blaine. I run the Crystal Chandelier over yonder.'

'It was indeed an agreeable surprise

to get my release from the new marshal of Wichita,' Jagus replied casually. 'What do you have in mind to fill our pockets with all that lovely *dinero, señor*?'

'Have the rest of the day to settle into your new roles, boys,' Blaine declared officiously to let these jaspers know exactly who was running this show. 'First thing in the morning we need to start persuading the other saloon owners that it will be in their best interests to sell up to Cody and me. You boys will be our muscle. Once the word gets passed around, Wichita will be buzzing with cowboys eager to spend their dough in our gambling joints.'

∗   ∗   ∗

He left the two Valdez boys, a phony smile pasted across the unctuous kisser. Haughty arrogance oozed from every orifice. Although he would have denied the accusation, it was clear that greasers, half breeds and Indians would not be on the invitation list to his forthcoming nuptials. For that was Perry Blaine's next destination. Now that the obstacle to his quest for the hand of Tilly Dumont had been removed, the lady in question had no reason to stall him any further.

The gaze of the two missing names from the anticipated celebration followed him down the street, scornful arrows of disdain spearing his back. 'That *gringo* is one jumped-up turkey, Miguel,' Chico growled out, his fists bunching in irritation.

'Have patience, *hermano*,' Miguel counselled, playfully tapping his brother's shoulder. 'All in good time. Once things are running smoothly, then we will turn the tables on these pumped-up roosters.'

The meeting next day took place in Cody Meek's office. Meek himself explained in detail how the other business establishments were going to be 'encouraged' to make the right decision. Sly smirks broadened into beaming grins as the plan was divulged.

First visitation on the wanted list was the Drovers' House. Wishbone Adderley was on the town council and a buddy of the allegedly deceased marshal. He did not employ any hard-assed minders to keep the punters in line. There was no need. Adderley had signed a temperance decree the previous year. It was pinned up behind the bar for all to see.

Alcoholic beverages were not on the menu. Coffee and sarsaparilla were the strongest drinks on offer.

'This will be a piece of cake, boys,' Meek instructed his entourage which comprised his two partners together with Browny Jagus and two other hard-boiled toughs on the payroll. 'If'n Adderley foolishly refuses to sign over his holding, the others will soon toe the line when they hear what happens to troublemakers.'

The six men had moved down into the bar of the Prairie Dog and were enjoying a final drink before setting off.

The downcast look on Perry Blaine's face was not what Meek expected from his partner.

'What's eating you?' Meek snapped out. 'You ought be straining at the leash to get all these lunkheads dancing to our tune.'

'It's Tilly. She's turned me down again.' Blaine was totally bewildered by the singer's rejection. 'What's wrong with that dame? I thought she loved me. Can't she see a good deal when it's staring her in the face?'

The uncomfortable confession elicited a barely controlled chuckle from Meek. 'Don't take it too badly,' he chided his partner. 'That dame is still grieving over her lost love. Once she sees all that dough you'll be making, she'll soon come round. They always do. Take my word for it. Ain't that so, boys?'

'Sure is, partner,' Lobo concurred, lighting up a cigar. He liked the sound of being able to call someone that. 'But love don't come into it. *Señoritas* always like the good things in life. And the *hombre* who gives them those good things can always call the shots.'

Blaine was wriggling in his seat. He hated the thought of having his innermost feelings discussed in public, especially by a damned half-breed. He pushed his chair back. 'Let's get this show on the road then,' he rasped, trying to shrug off his discomfiture.

The only person in the Drovers' House when the deputation arrived was Jimmy Juniper. 'Beat it, kid,' snarled a young tough called Billy Joe Crabtree. 'We have private business with the boss.'

Jimmy looked to the man standing behind the counter for instructions. 'Do like the man says, kid. I'll handle this.'

Somewhat reluctantly the boy sidled outside. But he was not happy. This did not look like a friendly visit. So he hung around outside.

Unfortunately, the window curtain rail was too high for a short dude like him to see over. He would have to try listening in to what was under discussion. But even that was to be denied him. The other hard ass known simply as Stonewall stumped across and slammed the door shut.

It was Cody Meek who had delegated himself to do all the talking. And he got straight down to business. An official looking piece of thick parchment was slapped down on the counter. It was all elegant scroll-writing complete with the red seal of approval from a friendly lawyer who was being well paid for his work.

'What's this?' Adderley snapped, peering down at the document.

'A bill of transfer for these premises to the Wichita Land Holding Commission,' Meek announced, holding the other man's gaze. 'And you can see that we're prepared to offer a suitable remuneration for your co-operation.' He pushed the document forward, his tone of voice adopting a brittle rasp. 'Now sign it!'

Adderley looked at the piece of

paper, then up at the grim looking delegation. 'And what if'n I don't want to sell up? The sum you're offering is daylight robbery, a fraction of what this place is worth.'

The atmosphere suddenly grew tense as the partners of the WLHC supported by their muscle closed in. 'This ain't a request, Adderley. It's an order. And should you refuse, there's a clause in there,' he tapped the document meaningfully, 'giving us the right to take it by compulsory purchase at a much lower price.'

'You can't do that, it's against the law,' the diner boss protested.

'We're the law in this town now. Marshal Bonner has resigned.' Sniggers from Lobo and his brother greeted this announcement. 'And these two guys have kindly stepped in at short notice to fill the breech.'

A heavy silence followed akin to that at a funeral.

'So are you going to sign or not? It's your call, mister.' Meek and the others stood waiting, hands poised menacingly above gun butts while Wishbone Adderley pondered on his limited choices.

'OK, you seem to have the whip hand here, I'll sign.' He reached down below the counter ostensibly to secure a pen. But his searching hand found the butt of a revolver kept there for trouble such as this.

The twitch in the corner of an eye gave him away. Lobo had seen such nervous indications many times from guys who figured they had the match of the hired gunman. He was still here to prove otherwise. His own weapon was palmed in an instant, blasting flame and death towards the naïve café owner. Adderley staggered back. The gun fell from his weak grasp as he disappeared behind the counter. The shriek of dismay from outside went unheeded.

'Now that was a foolish move, Mr Adderley,' remarked Meek, removing a pen from his jacket and scrawling a note in the place reserved for the seller's name. It read: BOUGHT BY

COMPULSORY PURCHASE. 'But it saves us having to hand out any dough.'

Perry Blaine turned towards the bodyguards. 'You boys spread the word. And make sure the owners of the other premises know what happens if'n they adopt the same high-handed attitude as poor old Wishbone.' He handed Billy Joe a list of five saloons, plus the gun shop and general store that needed their expertly persuasive talents. 'Take some more of the boys and let them know we'll be along shortly.'

By the end of the week, all of the town's principal businesses were in the hands of the self-appointed Land Commission. Only one saloon owner on the list had displayed any backbone when handed the ultimatum. Ellis Fargo who ran the Oriental had no intention of handing over his hard-earned business for a pittance. He barricaded himself inside the saloon and challenged the interlopers to do their worst.

'I'm ready for you skunks,' he called

out when the knock came on the locked front door. 'Try breaking in and I'll cut you to ribbons. There's enough ammo and food in here to last me a month. You ain't getting your dirty hands on the Oriental while there's breath in my body.'

'That can certainly be arranged, Fargo, if'n you don't see sense,' replied an irked Cody Meek. But there was to be no stand-down from the stubborn owner. Meek scowled at the locked door. But the delegation was forced to retreat to the opposite side of Kingman to discuss what to do next.

It was a stand-off. Shots were fired and threats made. But Fargo remained adamant that he was staying put. After half an hour of stalemate, the WLHC faction retired to the Prairie Dog to determine what action to take. A couple of hired toughs kept watch on the Oriental to make sure that Fargo stayed inside.

'No way can we let this critter off the hook,' Meek angrily remonstrated. 'He gets away with this and it might give the others some unwelcome ideas. We have to do something, and fast.'

Various ideas were tossed around but none were deemed practicable. Eventually it was left to the new marshal who suggested a way round the irksome dilemma. 'Reckon there's only one way to teach this varmint a lesson,' Lobo declared. The others waited for him to reveal his plan. 'Burn him out. The Oriental is the one place along Kingman that's not attached to any other. So the fire won't spread.'

'But that will destroy a going concern,' objected Blaine. 'And the Oriental does good business.'

Lobo scoffed at the impresario's hostility towards his plan. 'What's one saloon? You already have enough rope to tie this town up good and proper. Let Fargo win and it could put the kibosh on us all getting rich.'

'He's right, Perry,' Meek said, concurring with their new partner. 'We have to let everybody know who's running things around here. A burn-out will deliver that message loud and clear.'

And so it was agreed. They took up positions opposite the saloon. Meek made one final attempt to bring the defiant rebel to his senses. A spirited 'Go to Hell!' from Ellis Fargo was followed up by a fusillade of shots. But none found their mark. All the assailants kept their heads well down.

Browny Jagus couldn't resist a mocking taunt. 'That the best you can do, Fargo? If'n you think a few slugs are gonna frighten us off, you're one *estupido tonto*.'

'My brother just called you a foolish idiot, *señor*. You going to stand for that?'

More shots were followed by ribald laughter from the attackers. But the goading was a deliberate ploy to hold the attention of the renegade while Billy Joe and Stonewall slipped round the back to set the fire going beneath the raised foundations of the wooden structure.

Within minutes smoke was billowing out as the deadly conflagration took hold. Orange flames licked hungrily at the dry wood as the fire rapidly spread to the upper storey. Nobody cheered. It was a poignant reminder of how deadly a rampant fire can be. The attackers watched, mesmerized by the dancing flames as they waited for the trapped man to emerge.

'What in blue blazes is the fool doing in there?' exclaimed Perry Blaine.

'Maybe he wants an Indian send-off,' remarked Lobo with casual unconcern. 'Don't make no difference in the end.'

'There he is!' Jagus called out.

A figure had emerged onto the upper veranda. It was Ellis Fargo. His arms were flapping like crazy as he desperately tried to bat out the flames consuming his clothes. But there was no escape from the rampaging inferno. Lobo drew his pistol. 'That guy needs putting out of his misery.' This was no act of mercy on the part of the cold-eyed killer. He could have been shooting an injured dog. The shot was accurately placed, striking the burning figure dead centre.

Fargo plunged over the railing.

'Aaaaaaaaagh!!' The wail of terror was cut short when the human torch hit the dirt.

Lobo blew the smoke from his gun barrel and with a nonchalant smirk declared to one and all, 'Looks like the town's in our hands now, *amigos*.'

'Yahoooo!' cheered his brother. 'This deserves a drink or three to celebrate, *muchachos*.'

Billy Joe joined in the hallooing. 'I'm all for that. Let's go, fellas,' he said leading the way back up the street to the Prairie Dog, leaving the rampant blaze to burn itself out. Meek and Blaine followed behind effecting a more dignified bearing that accorded with their newly acquired status as the rulers of Wichita.

The reversal of circumstances affecting the town had stunned the regular citizens. Such was the rapidity of change they had been impotent to stop. Mayor Wishart, who had attempted to remonstrate with the hedonistic transformation, was brusquely pushed aside and removed from office. His formal regalia was commandeered by Cody Meek who had always hankered after becoming Mayor of Wichita.

His wish had now come true. Donning the ceremonial robe and chain of office he strutted around town. It provided a disturbing indication to one and all that the old order had passed.

The carpetbaggers who had set up shop over the river in Delano were equally dismayed. Their patrons soon abandoned the rough and ready establishments for those being resurrected in Wichita. A collective sigh of satisfaction tempered with relief was patiently evident as Meek and Blaine welcomed all comers.

Once again the universal cry was taken up — 'Anything goes in Wichita'.

11

Back from the Brink

While all this was taking place, Cal Bonner was laid up in Dead Man's Draw. It had been touch and go whether he would survive the first night. Nightjar had stayed at the cabin to tend the patient. 'Any sign of his deteriorating and I need to know,' the doctor had ordered his makeshift assistant. 'We should know in a couple of days if he's going to pull through.'

It was three days before Cal finally rejoined the land of the living. Nightjar fussed around making sure he didn't try getting up. 'The doc gave me strict orders to make sure you rest up to let those wounds heal properly. And I'm a man of my word.' He gently eased the sick man back onto the bed. 'I've made a pot of strong broth. You're gonna need building up to tackle those skunks who are running the town now.'

The loyal stableman went on to outline the course of events that had bypassed the unconscious lawman since his disastrous showdown with Lobo. But Cal's principal concern was for his wife. 'Does she know that I'm still alive?' he worriedly enquired.

Nightjar shook his head. 'Only me and the doc are in on this subterfuge,' the old timer said. 'He reckons that if'n Miss Tilly finds out, she'll let the cat out the bag. The fewer people who are in on this caper, the safer for you. If'n those jaspers find out you're still breathing, they'll shift heaven and earth to finish the job properly.'

Cal nodded morosely. It made sense. But his heart went out to the woman he loved. Her heart would be needlessly broken, and all because of those scheming rats. Once again he struggled to rise. But he was still far too weak, and flopped back onto the bed. 'Patience they tell me is a virtue,' chided the finger-wagging Nightjar. 'And you're gonna need a heap of that stuff before getting back into the saddle.'

A week passed before Cal Bonner felt strong enough to venture outside the confining walls of the small cabin. Sniffing the fresh air and watching the meadow larks cavorting playfully in the clearing was a tonic in itself. His first smoke in over a week made him cough, but the calming effect of the tobacco helped to focus his thoughts.

His right hand was still bandaged. The doc had sadly declared it unfit for purpose. He could shoot with both hands but the right had been essential for making a fast draw. Although it hadn't done him much good against Lobo. That was because the guy played dirty by not offering his opponent an even break. Cal had been caught unawares and paid the price. A naïve assumption that would not be repeated. It was only through Doc Bailey's quickwitted intervention that he had survived. He owed the guy a great deal. Nightjar too.

With his strength returning, Cal began practising with the left hand. He flexed the muscles, which felt stiff and awkward. 'You are gonna have to do the business now,' he quietly mumbled to the wriggling fingers.

Remote from the regular trail, Dead Man's Draw was an ideal spot. It was tough going at first. His movements were slow and clumsy. But he soon became more adept, the accuracy of his shooting more centralized and on target. Shooting with the left hand could never match that of the right. So he could never hope to outgun Lobo in a regular shootout. Even Browny Jagus would now have the edge.

There had to be some other way of gaining the advantage. Avenging the humiliation he had suffered at the hands of these varmints was now his number one priority. 'What's happening in town?' he asked the visiting doctor one day.

Bailey went on to elaborate how the town had reverted to its old ways. All the saloons had been forcibly grabbed by Cody Meek and his underlings. Ostensibly with legitimate deeds of transfer that weren't worth the paper they were printed on. But with Lobo and Browny Jagus now in charge of law and order, the town had been opened up to all and sundry.

The old days of mayhem and riotous behaviour had returned with a vengeance. Respectable folks huddled inside their homes when the cowboys hit town. And that was most of the time. More and more herds were coming up the trail from Texas. And their primary destination was Wichita.

'And what of my wife?' Cal ventured. 'How has she taken it? Does she miss me?' Cal's pleading eyes forced the medic to look away. This was the one question he had been dreading. The doc's hesitation was not lost on the questioner. 'If'n there's something I need to know, then best spit it out, Doc.'

Bailey swallowed. 'It ain't good news. She's decided that there's no future for her in Wichita. Too many harsh memories. You can't rightly blame her.'

Cal was devastated. Anger bit deep into his reaction to this dire revelation. 'All this is down to Meek and Blaine, the conniving rats. When is she planning to leave?'

'I tried to persuade her to stay on. But she figures to be on the next stage leaving at the end of the week.'

Cal's head slumped onto his chest. Desolation etched a path across a face ravaged by grief. The doctor's sympathetic gaze followed him as the distraught man walked away, contemplating a future where little now seemed to matter except making those critters pay. How that could be managed was to occupy his entire being for the next few days.

The key lay in removing the snake's head. In this case, that was the hired gunslinger known as Lobo. Apart from his right hand, the damaged frame was now almost back to full strength. Flexing the left hand elicited a fractious scowl. It would never be the same as the right but would have to suffice. Going up against Lobo and his brother alone was not a sensible option. In normal circumstances he might have been able to take them both down, knowing how their devious minds operated. Lobo was fast, no question about it. So he would need to adopt a different tactic. Be as devious as he was.

But what could it be? The conundrum was still unresolved when he decided to let his mind rest for a spell. Reading might help conjure up some ideas. Skinny Jim seemed to have been an avid reader. Probably due to him living out here all alone. A stack full of well-thumbed tomes had been left behind. But none appealed to Cal's restless spirit.

Then he saw an old newspaper. It was the *Brisbane Herald*, which appeared to infer that Jim Flint was from Australia. But what caught the reader's attention was the main headline that read: ANOTHER BANK ROBBERY BY THE INFAMOUS KELLY GANG. Underneath was a pen drawing of the leader Ned Kelly clad in a homemade suit of armour. Cal was soon engrossed in the latest lawless undertaking of this notorious Aussie brigand. It was not the guy's usurping of the law that held his attention, but his use of bullet-proof protection.

As he read on, an idea began to form in the avenger's brain. Could this be his answer to thwarting the gunslinging prowess of his main adversary? He would need to acquire a suitable chest plate to wear beneath his jacket, thus protecting his vital organs. Most killers aimed for the heart. It was a natural target. There was no reason to suppose that in a showdown, Lobo would not do the same yet again. It was pure luck last time that the gunman had only missed the old ticker by a whisker.

With his mind made up, and fully enthused by his plan, Cal filled Nightjar in on the scheme. 'You should have access to a suitable piece of strong metal. All I'll need to do is hammer it into shape then hang it around my neck. A buttoned-up jacket should hide it so as not to give the game away.'

The old guy was less enthusiastic. 'You sure about this, Marshal?' the ostler cautioned. 'That guy is more slippery than a wet trout.'

'I'll never beat him in a straight gunfight,' Cal snapped back, irked that the livery man had poured cold water on his plan. 'Not with my left hand. And this one will never be the same again.' He held up the right that was still bandaged. A look akin to that of a cornered puma was reflected in the glittering eyes.

'You're taking a big chance. These guys play for keeps.'

'And so do I, Nightjar. So do I,' came back the tetchy retort. 'Don't forget that I'll have surprise on my side. It'll knock the stuffing out of him knowing I ain't pushing up the daisies after all. That should give me an edge.' Cal smiled for the first time following his near-death experience. He was convinced that he had struck upon a solid plan. It felt good to have a purpose once more. And this time he would make sure to come out the winner.

On his next visit, Nightjar presented him with a couple of possible choices, only one of which was suitable. The metal of the other was too thin. The intended apparatus needed to be capable of stopping a .45 bullet at close quarters. He had also borrowed some cutting tools from the local blacksmith. 'Don't worry,' he mollified the younger man. 'I told him they were for some work I was doing in the stable.'

Cal was exceedingly grateful for the old timer's help. 'Don't mind me if'n I seem a mite tetchy at times,' he apologized, knowing some sharp words had been exchanged during his enforced recuperation. 'Don't know what I'd have done without your help. It's feeling so helpless. That's what gets a fella down.'

'Use me as a punch bag all you want, Marshal. I can take it,' Nightjar replied. 'Just so long as you know what you're doing.'

'Reckon this will be my best hope of cutting those varmints down to size.'

Over the next few days, Cal hammered and bent the hunk of metal — in essence an old water pail — into the right shape to fit his lean frame. Holes were drilled in the corners for the rope fastenings to keep the makeshift armour in position. The dress rehearsal was a total success.

Nightjar expressed a positive verdict on how the hidden protection looked. 'Nobody will be any the wiser that you're wearing a reshaped bucket under your coat. How does it feel?'

Cal walked around the clearing. 'A bit heavier than I expected but nothing I can't get used to. And I've shaped it

195

for easy access to my shooting irons.' He drew one of the Navy Colts in a cross draw with his left hand.

Nightjar gasped in unashamed awe. 'Gee, Marshal, that was fast. Reckon Lobo and his danged brother are in for the surprise of their lives.'

A look of restrained enthusiasm played across the other man's lined face. 'That's slow compared to what Lobo is capable of. That's why I need this backup.' He tapped the protective steel beneath his coat. It rang out, a clarion call to arms.

'So when's the big day?' Nightjar's tentative enquiry held a note of uncertainty.

'Reckon there's no time like the present. Best to get this over with as soon as possible.'

'What do you want me to do?' the willing participant eagerly asked.

'Keep out of the firing line,' Cal cautioned his loyal supporter. 'You done more than any guy could ask of you. Just sit back and watch a magician at work as he transforms a town back to what it should be. Those conniving chisellers are gonna receive the shock of their lives.'

12

The Lion's Den

Adele had risen early that final morning in Wichita. This was the day she would finally leave the town, never to return. There were still a couple of hours before the noon stage departed. And she intended to be on it. But first she wanted to pay a last visit to the one person in town who had shown her kindness with no ulterior motive. Marge Gillett had proved to be a true friend in need.

She was passing the Crystal Chandelier when Perry Blaine emerged. Adele cut him short before he had a chance to speak. 'Don't even try to persuade me to stay, Perry. There's nothing between us, and never was. It was all in your mind.'

'You could have had it all, Tilly.

Fame, fortune and enough dough to buy you the world.' The impresario sneered as he continued. 'But you had to choose a no-account badge-toter like Bonner. And now the skunk's dead. There's still time for you to change your mind.'

'Cal was more of a man than you'll ever be,' the woman lambasted the squirming libertine. 'And for your information, I told him straight that we had no future unless he abandoned this life. Your hired killer took that decision away from him. And for that I could never forgive you.' She turned her back and walked away. 'Don't bother to see me off. You won't be welcome.'

Halfway down the street, Doc Bailey intercepted her. 'I have something important to tell you,' he declared in a clandestine manner, taking her arm and leading her out of earshot down a side road. 'It's about Cal.'

'What could you possibly have to divulge at this late hour?' the woman stated impatiently. 'I'm busy. There's a lot to be settled before I leave town.' Nevertheless, she allowed herself to be detoured.

'You need to prepare yourself for a shock,' the medic whispered. Bailey looked around, wary that unwelcome ears might be flapping. Only the creaking of a loose door disturbed the tense silence.

'What's so important then?'

'Cal is still alive!' The woman blanched. Such a blunt statement was certainly a bolt from the blue. 'And he's coming to town this morning for a showdown with Lobo and the others. I couldn't tell you before because we needed to keep a lid on things while he recovered from the shooting in the Prairie Dog. But he's better now, and eager to put things right.'

Adele stopped and stared at the medic. The ashen look on her face betrayed a disquieting uncertainty resulting from the startling revelation. For a moment she was too stunned to respond. Bailey gave her time to assimilate the momentous tidings.

'So why tell me now?'

'Everybody knows you are intending to leave Wichita today. So I felt it only right that you should reconsider such a drastic step now you know the situation.' Bailey was sure in his own mind that Adele would be overjoyed on learning her husband was still in the land of the living.

Her stony regard was not the reaction he expected.

'What's with the glum face, Adele? Anybody would think you didn't welcome your husband's resurrection from the dead. It's a miracle that should be celebrated.' His own response was terse and held the hint of accusation. 'Is it Blaine? Have you already accepted his offer of marriage?'

Such an allegation brought the colour back into Adele's face. She bristled with indignation. 'If you must know I've given that manipulative toad the brush-off. Cal was only ever the one for me. But if he isn't prepared to walk away from all this, there can be no future for us. I've had enough waiting up for a man who seems intent on forever putting his life on the line. My mind is made up.' She looked directly at the medic, challenging him to dispute her decision. 'Sure, I'm relieved that he's survived. But it doesn't change anything for me. And I aim to be on the stage when it leaves today.'

Bailey was equally forthright. 'You disappoint me, Adele. I had you down as a loyal wife, a woman with backbone and the guts to stand up for what is right. A woman who was prepared to back her man to the hilt no matter what the outcome. All you're doing is running away. You've done it before. So go on, leave. You don't deserve a man like Cal Bonner.' And with that final denunciation, he walked away without looking back.

Adele just stood there, perplexed and hesitant. The doctor's curt indictment had left her questioning her actions. Was she being disloyal? A timid mouse rather than the feisty strong-willed performer she portrayed on stage? Wrapped in a cloud of wavering vacillation, she wandered aimlessly eventually arriving outside Marge Gillett's rooming house.

Here was one woman who might understand her plight. She knocked on the door. The lady in question opened up and let her in with a smile. 'I was hoping you'd come by afore shipping out,' the widow enthused, ushering her guest into the parlour. 'I was just gathering Cal's things together. Maybe you can tell me if'n he had any kin who might want them?'

'There won't be any need for that, Marge.'

'What do you mean?' the older woman asked quizzically while pouring the tea.

'He's still alive. The bullets missed his heart by a whisker.'

Adele's astonishing pronouncement left Marge bewildered. But she soon recovered, declaring excitedly, 'So you won't be leaving after all. I'm so glad.

The pair of you were made for each other . . . '

A raised hand cut off the woman's gushing flow. 'I still intend to be on the stage at noon. Doc Bailey has told me Cal is itching to settle the score with Cody Meek and his bunch. I want no part of any more gunplay.'

The widow's beaming smile fell away like melted ice cream off a spoon. 'I'm sorry about that, Adele. You're letting yourself down. But more importantly, you're letting Cal down. He does this job to keep the rest of us safe from harm. That's all he has ever wanted. It's the lawless elements, the gunslingers and carpet-baggers who want to take over and create mayhem. Cal and those other brave souls like him have made the West a place to call home, where people can be happy and set down roots without fearing for their lives. He has placed his life on the line many times to keep this town safe for good-living folk.'

Adele raised her hand to stop the reproving flow.

But Marge was not to be silenced. Her voice rose as the tongue-lashing reached its climax. 'Land sakes, girl,' she exclaimed hotly. 'Have you no shame, abandoning the guy in his hour of need?'

Adele was visibly shaken by the outburst. She had listened intently. Never previously had she thought of it in those terms. Perhaps as Marge Gillett inferred, she was being selfish. She sat down and drank her tea. There was much to think on. Much to mull over. This woman and Doc Bailey had placed their faith in Cal Bonner to bring order out of chaos, harmony out of discord. Didn't such a man deserve her full support?

'You have certainly given me a lot to think about, Marge,' she pondered, standing up to depart. 'Maybe I have been looking at the world from the wrong angle, one of self-interest instead of considering the common good. And what that means to Cal.'

Her mind a welter of confused feelings, Adele wandered back to her room at the hotel. Her bags were packed. The rest of the entourage had already left for the next engagement in Hayes City. Would Tilly Dumont be joining them?

★   ★   ★

Normally discreet when it came to confidences, on this occasion Nightjar felt the marshal was taking on more than he could chew. The stableman had ridden hard back from Dead Man's Draw. Cal Bonner needed help if'n he was to turn the tables on Lobo and the others. Challenging a whole town on his ownsome was asking for that wooden overcoat he had barely avoided the last time they met. There were others in town who would back his play. But only if'n they thought there was a good chance of ousting the lowlifes and chisellers who had taken over.

206

Argo Creede was always grumbling. Now was his chance to do something about it by supporting the marshal. Then there was the expelled mayor, Henry Wishart. He would surely want to even the score with those skunks who so humiliated him. Doc Bailey was also an obvious supporter. And others would surely come out of the woodwork when word got around that Bear River Cal was back.

Nightjar wasted no time in putting his plan into action. Doc Bailey was his first port of call. Once apprised of the situation and knowing that time was of the essence, the medic quickly summoned a meeting of all those he knew were of a like mind.

And so it was that when Cal Bonner arrived on the outskirts of Wichita he was met by a small deputation numbering ten supporters. The marshal was visibly moved by the show of collaboration. He had been prepared to go it alone. But knew that he was placing his head in the lion's mouth with every possibility of having it bitten off.

Nevertheless he still wanted to prove he had the courage and guts to face down any opposition; be seen as the man in charge. 'I sure appreciate you folks backing me up,' he declared, noticeably enthused by the presence of these people. 'But I don't want anybody putting their lives in danger for me. Only make your presence felt if'n these rats decide to play dirty. It's important that I make them see who's in charge. Not Blaine or Meek, but Cal Bonner. I've done it before, and I can do it again. Remember, if'n we succeed, I have to make it stick in the future.'

A sigh of relief issued from a few of the more wary supporters, men who hated the current rule of anarchy but felt inadequate when it came to a physical confrontation. Cal didn't blame them. Not everybody was as mule-headed as him. So he offered them an olive branch. 'I'm more than grateful for your presence. Just showing these jaspers that there are still plenty of decent folk living in Wichita is enough for me.'

'We'll back you up with these if'n it comes to the crunch,' professed Nightjar waving an old Colt Dragoon in the air. 'Won't we, boys?' A murmur of concurrence rippled through the gathering.

'We'll start with the Troubadour,' Cal declared, stepping forth in the lead of the unofficial posse. 'You boys stay outside. Keep a sharp lookout through the window. Only come in if'n you see that I'm in trouble.' A nod of agreement rippled through the thin ranks.

A deep breath, a girding of resolve filtered down through the lean, rangy frame. Inside the saloon, a jangling piano was being battered into submission by a drunken cowboy. His buddies were all jigging around in wild abandon. And it was only ten o'clock in the morning.

'This is what we're faced with all day, everyday, including Sunday,' Mayor Wishart grumbled. 'Soon they'll tumble outside and start racing up and down the street firing off their guns.'

'And this is only one saloon,' added the morose figure of Nathan Clover, the bank manager. 'There's been another three opened up since you were shot down.'

'Then I have a lot to do,' Cal replied, oozing a confidence he hoped was being communicated to his associates. And with that he stepped briskly into the lion's den.

13

Spellbound!

With a loaded shotgun in one hand and Navy Colt in the other, Bear River Cal stood in the doorway. His profile cast a long shadow down the middle of the saloon floor. For a moment nobody noticed the newcomer. But they soon got the message that things were about to change, radically. The shotgun blasted a hole in the ceiling. Plaster and broken lathes cascaded over nearby drinkers. Everybody turned quickly to see what had caused the cacophony.

Cal didn't give them any chance to voice objections. One raucous cowpoke nudged by his buddy stumbled too close to the perpetrator of the mayhem. His reward was a gun butt over the head, which floored him. 'As from now, this saloon is closed for business until further notice. Any objections should be addressed to my friend here.'

The lethal shotgun wafted menacingly in the faces of those nearest. They instantly cowered back. 'I'm resuming my duties as marshal of this town as from now.' A defiant gaze panned the room seeking out any dissension.

A bartender called Spider Jones made the mistake of moving to his right where a pistol was concealed beneath the bar. With everybody else stunned into silence and frozen to the spot, the move was easy to detect. Cal allowed the sneaky critter to palm the gun and raise it above the bar. A shot rang out. The hole in his forehead was plumb centre. Jones crashed back, his windmilling arms displacing a pile of glasses. The crash of splintering glass found the whole throng retreating as the perpetrator slowly advanced.

'Anybody else have a beef against this, tell the mayor who is also resuming his official duties.' He called over his shoulder. 'OK boys, you can come in and take over. The Troubadour is now officially closed.' Such was the rapid reversal of fortunes, that nobody voiced any further opposition. 'And you can tell anybody else you meet that Lobo and Browny Jagus have just resigned . . . permanently.'

Cal's supporters immediately began ushering the subdued patrons out into the street. 'You boys want any more action, you'll have to cross the river to Delano,' Nightjar obligingly informed the stunned cowboys.

No further time was wasted on the Troubadour as Cal marched off up the street to the next den of iniquity. His success in the first saloon had buoyed up his self-belief. While Mayor Wishart and the others were sealing off the Troubadour, a few other residents began emerging from their stores to join the lawman.

'Gee, Marshal,' exclaimed Ike Robbins who ran the saddlery. 'We all thought you were dead and gone. Is it really you?'

'Sure is, boys. And I'm back in business. Are you ready to back my play?'

'Never more so,' butted in Smoky Joe, the tobacconist. 'This town has gone to the dogs since Lobo took over as marshal. If'n you can get rid of Cody Meek and his bunch, there'll be free Havanas for a year.'

'That go for me as well, Smoky?' piped up Nightjar hopefully.

'Dream on, old timer. That offer is a one-off for the man in charge.'

Forced chuckles soon dissolved as the magnitude of their task permeated through to the core of each man there. One after another of the gambling joints, hen houses and saloons operated by Meek's underlings surrendered to the blunt effectiveness of Cal Bonner's town-taming proficiency.

Word quickly spread like a rampant prairie fire that the marshal was back in business. Ham-like fists in conjunction with the more usual hardware ploughed a furrow across the town's wayward decadence. It was Billy Joe Crabbe who brought the disquieting news to the main perpetrators. He burst unannounced into Meek's office upstairs in the Prairie Dog.

'Don't you ever think of knocking before busting into my office?' the gambler scowled jumping to his feet. 'This is a private meeting you're butting in on.' The two men had been assessing the profits accrued since the town had been thrown open to all comers.

The tough ignored the rebuke. 'It's Bonner. He's back, and causing a heap of trouble . . . '

Blaine interjected with a cutting retort. 'What in hell's name are you blathering on about? Bonner's dead and buried.'

Crabbe shook his head. 'I tell you he's closing down all our joints.' The ruffian's panic-stricken declaration caught their attention. 'And he's got the backing of Wishart and the other lunkheads on the council. They'll be here soon. What are we gonna do about it?'

The stunning news had thrown them completely off guard. Only Lobo appeared unphased. The gunman eased himself out of the easy chair where he had been lounging. His eyes narrowed to thin slits of ice. He knew where this was heading. 'It's obvious, ain't it?' he snarled while checking the load of his six shooter. 'That sawbones hoodwinked us when he declared that Bonner was dead.' A rabid curse burst from between pursed lips. 'And I fell for it.'

Meek immediately took control of the escalating panic that was gripping his associates. 'This is where you earn your partnership, Lobo. I brought you in here to make certain that critter didn't cause us any more trouble. You failed. This is a second chance to make things right. Do it properly this time.'

Lobo stiffened. 'Don't you threaten me, *hombre*.'

His brother interjected before the

disagreement got out of hand.

'He's right, Miguel. This is our chance to take that interfering *zorrillo* out once and for all,' Browny Jagus iterated eagerly. 'The two Valdez brothers acting as a team. What could be better? We'll be famous. Nobody will dare challenge us once word spreads across the territory how we bested Bear River Cal Bonner. What do you say?'

Lobo smiled, impulsively rubbing the tin star on his chest. Yellow teeth bared in the grin of a rampant wolf. 'I like it, Chico,' he concurred, making for the door. 'Let's go have us a replay. And this time there'll be no mistake.'

Cal knew that his final destination had to be the Prairie Dog. This was where he had been brought low. That trace of arrogance, the notion that he had become invincible had almost cost him his life. No more. Now he was well aware of the danger about to be faced head on. But face it he must.

Over on the far side of Kingman, Adele rung her hands as the man she

217

had failed drew ever closer to the final countdown. Their eyes met. A brief melding of souls flitted across the dusty space. A moment of understanding. Then it was gone. There was work to be done. And all of the Bear River hero's nerve would be put to the test in the next few minutes.

He paused at the alley adjoining the saloon where Nightjar was waiting with his magician's props. The old guy had transported the armour plating in his wagon prior to Cal's arrival in town. He now helped the marshal don the cumbersome rigout.

'You sure about this?' was the ostler's concerned last-minute entreaty. 'There are enough of us to put the lid on any trouble now.'

Cal spurned the offer. This was his business, and his alone. 'Never more so, old timer. You just keep out the way along with these other folks. This is between me and Lobo now.' And with that final certitude, he stepped forward to meet his destiny.

Pausing inside the saloon to adjust his vision to the dim atmosphere, his body tensed, hands bent like claws ready to make the draw of his life. Two men faced him at the far end of the room. Lobo and Browny Jagus slowly moved forward. It was the older Valdez who broke the silence.

'Seems like you have more lives than a cat, *gringo*,' he snarled out. 'Well this is where the cat gets hung out to dry. Make your play.'

But his brother, dragging at the leash to get even, drew first. His shot blasted apart the heavy stillness. It was accurately placed and punched the victim back a couple of paces. But Cal did not go down. The old bucket armour had done its job. His own gun palmed, he returned fire.

Jagus staggered back under the impact of the lead balls. He clutched the bar top, hung there a moment, eyes wildly trying to figure out what had happened. His shots had struck the guy dead centre. But he was still on his feet.

How could that be? Jagus was not given the chance to further analyse the uncanny cause. A third shot finished him off. The killer slid to the floor and stayed there.

Lobo cursed the impulsiveness of his brother. But he likewise was momentarily taken aback. Cal gave him no time to cogitate. 'Always aim for the heart, Lobo,' he hissed out, moving forward catlike. 'That's the only way you can take me down.'

The gunman took the advice. Three shots blasted out. The strange ringing noise from the sure-fire hits failed to register as the renaissance man continued his slow advance down the room. 'What in tarnation is going on here?' Lobo yelled as he backed off.

'You didn't go for the heart, Lobo,' came back the casual reply. 'That's gonna cost you.' Cal raised his gun and let fly. Lobo's punctured body twisted round like a child's spinning top. 'This time it's me that's holding a winning hand and I'm calling in the chips.'

Cal stood over the fallen gunslinger. 'H-how did you m-manage it?' Lobo's weak plea for clarification was smilingly revealed as Cal unbuttoned his jacket.

'No magic. Just a bit of thoughtful defence against a couple of devious critters that don't understand the meaning of a straight shoot-out.'

Lobo's eyes bulged before rolling up into his head as he slid over to join his brother. Cal just stood there. His taut frame relaxed. But then he realized that this was not yet over. Not by a long shot. There still remained the two bastards who had hired this piece of scum. He was instantly reminded of their presence by movement on the floor above the saloon bar.

The time for skulduggery was over. He discarded the armour plating that had effectively done its job and backed away towards the door to reload his used Colt. He needed time to take stock of how to outfox those crafty shysters.

Hidden from view by a velvet

curtain, Stonewall was mesmerized by what he had just witnessed. The tough had been despatched by his boss to observe the gunfight from the upper landing. And if necessary to intervene. The bodyguard had his own views on that course of action. If Lobo and his brother could not contain the illusive marshal, he sure had no intention of taking him on.

His eyes widened in shock on seeing their enemy brashly chop down the two Valdez brothers cool as you please, and without a mark on his own body. Stonewall's hand was shaking. This guy must have a guardian angel looking out for him. He hurried back to the office to relay the startling information.

'Lobo was . . . he and Jagus were . . . '

'Spit it out, you idiot,' railed Meek angrily. 'What in thunderation are you burbling on about?'

Stonewall gulped. 'Bonner just cut the two of 'em down without any trouble,' the dazed minion muttered. 'And not a single one of their bullets

222

had any effect. The guy ain't human.'

Billy Joe Crabbe was equally worried at this sudden change of circumstances. Things were getting too darned hot to handle. He and his buddy had not signed up for this. Bonner was out for blood, their blood. And Billy Joe had every intention of keeping his own share of the red stuff inside his taut frame. A look of accord passed between the two underlings.

'We're pulling out, Cody,' Crabbe said, edging towards the door.

'This guy is too darned good for us,' his partner added, following.

'I'm sorry to hear that, boys,' Meek rasped angrily. Then a cunning smirk creased his face. 'But if'n you can't handle him, there's the door.' Blaine gave the remark a puzzled frown. This wasn't like Cody. Nobody walked out on him without payback. It came sooner than expected.

The two men gratefully thanked their employer as they hustled across the room. Crabbe grasped the door handle.

But he never managed to open it. A slug from the hidden pocket pistol drilled into Crabbe's back. The second shot took Stonewall out before he had time to register the dire peril the two pals had unwittingly instigated.

Meek blew away the smoke issuing from the twin barrels of the tiny gun. 'Nobody pulls out on Cody Meek without my say-so.'

Like the two underlings, Blaine was also greatly disturbed by the blunt challenge to their domination. It had all happened so fast. One minute they were discussing the erection of a new dance hall, the next, that surreal lawman was tearing their plans to shreds. 'It's right though what Stone-wall said, Cody,' Blaine mumbled nervously. 'That guy ain't of this world. I reckon it's time for us to split the breeze before this whole shebang comes crashing down about our ears.'

'Guess you're right there, Perry,' Meek agreed, hustling across to the wall safe. 'And now he's gotten the council off their asses, the future don't look rosy anymore for us in Wichita. We've made enough dough to set up some place else. I hear tell there's a place further west called Dodge City that's starting to attract attention.'

'Good idea. I'll go saddle the horses while you bag up the dough,' Blaine said, going out the back way. He had an emergency bag packed in his quarters above the theatre for circumstances such as this.

14

The Worm Turns

'Looks like we have the town under our control once again,' Mayor Wishart declared as he and the others joined the town tamer outside the Prairie Dog. 'And it's all down to you, Cal.'

But the official's euphoria was short-lived. Suddenly a couple of shots from inside the saloon found them all hitting the deck. They had clearly come from the upper storey. 'It's not over yet,' the marshal remarked, peering through the window. Nothing moved inside. No ghosts of resurrected gunslingers walked the boards. 'Looks like Meek and his cronies are fighting among themselves.'

'That's good for us, ain't it?' Smoky Joe said breezily.

'Not until every last one of those

critters is eating dirt or clapped behind bars,' Cal solemnly iterated. 'My job isn't over yet, boys.'

'You will be careful, won't you Cal?' The dulcet tones set the town tamer's heart racing. 'I'd hate for us to be parted again.' His head turned as the gathering moved apart to give them space. 'How can you ever forgive me for being so selfish?'

All Cal could see was that lovely face framed by tumbling auburn tresses. Eyes like twinkling stars drew him in. 'It'll all be over soon, honey,' he gulped. A croaking whisper struggled to voice his thoughts. 'Then we can be together. And I promise to change my ways.'

But first there was the thorny matter of stopping those crooks from escaping justice. With the greatest of reluctance he gently edged her away into the waiting arms of Marge Gillett. 'Keep her safe for me,' were his final words. The widow nodded. A long-awaited meeting of minds, then he disappeared back inside the saloon.

Left to his own devices for a while, Blaine began to have doubts regarding his partner. Cody Meek was a ruthless predator who wouldn't hesitate to toss his associates to the wolves should circumstances dictate. A self-serving villain with no scruples. Blaine's own shallow character went unheeded as his fertile mind began to conjure up the notion that Meek had all the dough and was intending to keep it.

Furtive eyes flickered around the empty theatre. Even now the varmint could be lying in wait, itching to gun him down. 'Well you ain't gonna get the better of me, buster,' he railed angrily at the silent auditorium. He checked his gun to ensure it was fully loaded then cat-footed across the stage and down through the dressing rooms to the back door. And there he waited. Gun clutched tightly in his fist, Perry Blaine's whole body tensed on hearing the approach of his allegedly cheating partner.

Hate oozed from every pore of his

being as the back door to the saloon opened and Meek stepped outside. Blaine was ready for him. 'Thought you could outfox me, didn't you Cody?' he snarled, pointing the gun at the saloon owner's back. 'Take all that dough for yourself. Well I'm onto your game.'

'What in blue blazes are you talking about?' Meek innocently protested. 'We're partners, ain't we? I'd never run out on you.'

'You won't get the chance, buddy.' His gun barked twice. Meek was punched forward. He never stood a chance. Whether or not he intended to fleece his partner would never see the light of day. He was dead. Blaine wasted no time in idly speculating on the truth. He snatched up the saddle bag containing the money and mounted up.

Inside the Prairie Dog, Cal was gingerly climbing the stairs. No sound could be heard. He had to assume the worst; that the two charlatans were lying in wait to chop him down. Peering round the edge of the upper corridor, he could see that the door to Cody Meek's private office was open. With the Navy Colt leading the way, he crept stealthily along the empty corridor, steps muffled by the thick carpet.

A quick peak around the door revealed the bodies of the two hard cases. The reason behind their sudden death went unheeded. Cody and Meek had clearly fled the scene.

He was considering how best to tackle the miscreants when two shots rang out. And they had come from the alley behind the saloon. Throwing caution to the wind, he dashed along to the back door and lurched out onto the veranda. There, lying in a pool of his own blood down below, was Meek. And he clearly would not be getting up. The drumming of hoof beats assailed his ears. A quick glance up the alley and he perceived a rider disappearing round the far corner.

It was Perry Blaine. The two worms had turned on one another and Blaine had come out the winner. But not for long, if Bear River Cal Bonner had anything to do with it. No need for prudence anymore. He dashed back down to the front of the saloon where his horse was tethered.

'What was all the shooting about, Cal?' the mayor asked. 'We thought you might have run into trouble.'

'Meek and Blaine have had a disagreement. And I'm going after the winner,' he shouted back while leaping into the saddle. Other questions were thrown his way, but they dissolved in the cloud of dust produced by the galloping cayuse.

Unseen by the mayor and those hovering outside the Prairie Dog, Blaine had crossed Kingman further down. Only two other people were walking along the opposite side of the street. Blaine's eyes widened. One was Marge Gillett who was accompanied by none other than Tilly Dumont. And they were about to enter the rooming house. Here was his ace in the hole. A chance to keep any pursuit by that interfering lawman at bay.

He dragged his horse to a halt beside the pair of ladies. 'You're coming with me, Tilly. And don't try any tricks. If'n I can't have you then nobody can.'

The girl was roughly hoisted across the saddle in front of Blaine. A heavy duty cuff round the head soon terminated any resistance to the abduction. But Marge Gillett had been raised on a dirt farm and was tough as old boots. She flung herself at the mounted rider clawing at his legs, trying to unseat him. 'Take your hands off'n her,' she snapped out, desperation evident in her fearful cry.

Blaine was not about to be cheated at this crucial stage by any damned females. His left boot lifted and drove the scrabbling widow off where she tumbled into a pool of muddy water. Free of any further encumbrance, he dug in the spurs and galloped off.

Marge lumbered to her feet, dripping

wet with clods of foul-smelling ordure clinging to her dress. But except for hurt pride, she was uninjured. A spirited dash along Kingman followed. Marge had never run so hard in her life. Her vigorous hollering attracted numerous strange comments from folks who had emerged from their homes anxious to determine the cause of all the shooting.

'Marshal Bonner, come quick!' she yelled out, frantically waving her hands. 'Perry Blaine has kidnapped Tilly. You have to go after them quick.'

Cal reined in on the corner opposite the saddlery. 'Take it easy, Marge,' he taxed the agitated woman. 'No reason for you to bust a blood vessel.'

But the older woman was not to be placated. 'Get after that skunk lickety-spit. He's heading east along the road to Dead Man's Draw.' She paused to draw in a gulp of air. 'Clubbed the girl out cold with his meaty fist. I tried to stop him. But you can see what happened.'

She indicated the dire state of her muddy attire.

'Like the first day you arrived in Wichita. Remember? You should catch them up easy seeing as they're riding double.'

Blaine realized that he could never outrun Cal Bonner while toting the woman along. But he knew exactly how to work this to his advantage. At the entrance to the Draw, he reined up and dragged Tilly off the horse. A few slaps around the kisser soon brought her round. 'Now listen up, girl,' he growled out. No longer the ardent lover, here was the real Perry Blaine: a hard-nosed thug who had no scruples when it came to saving his own skin. 'You're gonna be my ace up the sleeve to get that meddling tinstar off'n my back.'

A rough arm encircled her neck. The other hand held a gun to her head. They did not have long to wait. Within minutes, the stomp of pounding hoof beats lifted a cloud of dust from the far side of a low rise. Man and horse crested the rise but were forced to a stumbling halt by the terrifying sight of his true love in the intimidating clutches of her brutish oppressor.

'That's as far as you go, Bonner,' the rat sang out, jabbing the gun into his victim's cheek. 'Now step down and unbuckle your gunbelt then toss it aside. And make it slow and easy. One false move and the girl dies.'

Cal had been given no choice but to comply. 'You won't get away with this, Blaine. And even if'n you do, I'll hunt you down and feed your body to the hogs. Harm one hair of her head and you're dead meat.'

A mirthless cackle echoed around the rocky point. 'Toothless threats, Bonner. I'm the one giving the orders. Now shuck your boots and start walking back to town.'

Unfortunately for the aggressor, his whole attention was focused on ensuring that any threat from Bonner was neutralized. Adele took the bull by the horns and bit down on the arm now covering her mouth. Sharp teeth split the skin, drawing blood. The shock threw Blaine into a panic as he pulled his arm away. The pressure of his embrace slackened allowing Adele to wriggle free.

Cal wasted no time. He dived across to where his guns lay. Blaine snapped off a couple of shots. But he was no gunslinger and they went wide. Cal lay on the ground spread-eagled, his left hand cocking and firing the Navy Colt until the hammer clicked on empty. Six shots in all, of which four had struck their target. Blaine lay splayed out in the dust.

Staggering across, the man from Bear River stood over the corpse ready to despatch the full load of his other gun should the need arise. Ribs heaving as the blood pounded in his chest, he sank to his knees. It had been a close call. And he had Adele to thank for bringing this whole sorry episode to a suitable climax.

The girl hurried across and threw her

arms around the man she loved more than life itself. Both their lives had been spared. Surely that must be a sign from above that they were meant to stay together.

Cal slowly removed the badge from his chest and tossed it on the ground. 'I'm finished with this life, Adele. If'n you want me to tend store, then so be it. Anything to have you by my side.'

The girl held his face. Then she picked up the discarded star and pinned it back on his vest. 'No, Cal. This is what you do.' A soft hand caressed his stubble-coated cheeks. 'Marge and Doc Bailey opened my eyes. It made me realize how proud I am to call myself the wife of Marshal Cal Bonner, the man who tamed Wichita and brought peace so that good folks could walk the streets in safety.'

Then she kissed him full on the lips. Meadow larks chirruped with joy, a coyote howled its own accord. And peace had returned to Sedgwick County, thanks to the Wichita town tamer.

We do hope that you have enjoyed reading this large print book.

Did you know that all of our titles are available for purchase?

We publish a wide range of high quality large print books including:
Romances, Mysteries, Classics
General Fiction
Non Fiction and Westerns

Special interest titles available in large print are:
The Little Oxford Dictionary
Music Book, Song Book
Hymn Book, Service Book

Also available from us courtesy of Oxford University Press:
Young Readers' Dictionary
(large print edition)
Young Readers' Thesaurus
(large print edition)

For further information or a free brochure, please contact us at:
Ulverscroft Large Print Books Ltd.,
The Green, Bradgate Road, Anstey,
Leicester, LE7 7FU, England.
Tel: (00 44) **0116 236 4325**
Fax: (00 44) **0116 234 0205**

Other titles in the
Linford Western Library:

CHISHOLM TRAIL
SHOWDOWN

Jack Tregarth

For the young men in the Texas town of Indian Falls, riding the Chisholm Trail as cowboys is a rite of passage. Dan Lewis is heartbroken when it looks as though he is to be cheated of his chance. Determinedly, he manages to secure a place on the trail, but his joy quickly fades as he is accused of cattle rustling and nearly lynched. As he fights to clear his name, he finds himself up against a gang of the most ruthless men in the state . . .

LAND OF THE SAINTS

Jay Clanton

It is the summer of 1858, and the Turner family are making their way along the Oregon Trail to California. The wagon train with which they are travelling is attacked by a band of Paiute, but this is no mere skirmish in the Indian Wars. The territory of Utah, or Deseret as those who live there call it, is in open rebellion against the government in Washington. Turner and his wife and daughter are caught in the crossfire of what is turning out to be a regular shooting war.

FLAME ACROSS THE LAND

Colin Bainbridge

Fark Seaton comes to the aid of old timer Utah Red when he and his flock of sheep are attacked. Who is responsible? The evidence seems to point towards Mitch Montgomery and his Lazy Ladder outfit; but as tension mounts and the bullets fly, Seaton is not so sure. What is the role of Nash Brandon, owner of the Mill Iron? Could Seaton's interest in Montgomery's daughter, Maisie, be clouding his judgement? When the sparks of anger finally blaze into uncontrolled fury, the answers at last begin to emerge.